"I DON'T THINK I NEED TO ELABORATE ON WHY YOU ANNOY ME," SHE SAID COLDLY.

Rand frowned. "What are you talking about?"

"I'll tell you exactly what I'm talking about. You're so used to getting your own way. I guess it's only natural for some powerful, wealthy men to think they can make decisions for the entire world."

"Is that what you thought when I asked you to marry me, Jordon? Did you think I was trying to run your life?" he asked stiffly.

"Frankly, Rand, when you proposed, I was in shock over Dad's death. I would have agreed to just about anything. You were his friend, and I allowed you to control my life. That was a mistake, and in the end I was forced to assert myself."

"Assert yourself?" Rand's eyes narrowed into icy slits. "Is that what you call sleeping with Jason Mateo?"

CANDLELIGHT ECSTASY CLASSIC ROMANCES

QUANTITY SALES

Most Dell Books are available at special quantity discounts when purchased in bulk by corporations, organizations, and special-interest groups. Custom imprinting or excerpting can also be done to fit special needs. For details write: Dell Publishing Co., Inc., 1 Dag Hammarskjold Plaza, New York, NY 10017, Attn.: Special Sales Dept., or phone: (212) 605-3319.

INDIVIDUAL SALES

Are there any Dell Books you want but cannot find in your local stores? If so, you can order them directly from us. You can get any Dell book in print. Simply include the book's title, author, and ISBN number, if you have it, along with a check or money order (no cash can be accepted) for the full retail price plus 75¢ per copy to cover shipping and handling. Mail to: Dell Readers Service, Dept. FM, P.O. Box 1000, Pine Brook, NJ 07058.

TRIPLE THREAT

Eleanor Woods

A CANDLELIGHT ECSTASY ROMANCE®

Published by
Dell Publishing Co., Inc.
1 Dag Hammarskjold Plaza
New York, New York 10017

Dell ® TM 681510, Dell Publishing Co., Inc.

Candlelight Ecstasy Romance®, 1,203,540, is a registered trademark of Dell Publishing Co., Inc., New York, New York.

ISBN: 0-440-18823-7

Printed in the United States of America

November 1986

10 9 8 7 6 5 4 3 2 1

WFH

To Our Readers:

We have been delighted with your enthusiastic response to Candlelight Ecstasy Romances®, and we thank you for the interest you have shown in this exciting series.

In the upcoming months we will continue to present the distinctive sensuous love stories you have come to expect only from Ecstasy. We look forward to bringing you many more books from your favorite authors and also the very finest work from new authors of contemporary romantic fiction.

As always, we are striving to present the unique, absorbing love stories that you enjoy most—books that are more than ordinary romance. Your suggestions and comments are always welcome. Please write to us at the address below.

Sincerely,

The Editors
Candlelight Romances
1 Dag Hammarskjold Plaza
New York, New York 10017

TRIPLE
THREAT

CHAPTER ONE

Jordon Maxwell hurried down the aisles of Dupree's Family Grocery. Though petite and fragile-looking, she manned the grocery cart with confidence, her arms shooting out like deft robotic levers, grabbing a can of this, a box of that, from the shelves. Thank heavens, she sighed, there were hardly any other customers in the store to detain her.

Normally she enjoyed grocery shopping; New Orleans was a culinary haven, from the newest supermarkets to the small neighborhood stores that had become as much a part of the bustling city as its history. Today, however, there was a frown of sorts on Jordon's attractive face as her brown eyes caught a glimpse of her watch during one of her snatch-and-grab exercises. Already five forty-five. Darn! She shook her dark head defeatedly. She had only an hour to get home, unload the groceries, and then be back at the office in time to spend a few personal moments alone with the two new girls she was hiring. Jordon went to a great deal of time and trouble to give her customers the best service possible, and it was imperative that the two girls she was going to hire be very much aware of that fact. Jordon, twenty-seven years old and the mother of triplets, had worked like a slave to make her small business a success. Personal Shoppers might sound simple, but shopping and making selections for other people too busy to shop for themselves was time-consuming and required great doses of determination.

"I'll never make it on time." She moaned with a heavy sigh.

Her comment was heard by an elderly gentleman standing at the cheese section of the dairy counter. He smiled, then let his gaze linger pleasantly on the remarkably attractive face with warm brown eyes. Her figure was small and graceful from the top of her shoulder-length dark brown hair to the taupe pumps she was wearing. Nice to see a woman in a dress, he thought. Especially one with such good-looking legs.

Jordon, unaware of her elderly admirer, bent over to pick up a carton of eggs at the exact same second a loud noise was heard toward the front of the store. The peculiar sound was followed by the sharp *ping* of something hitting the metal backdrop of the refrigerated dairy shelves with tremendous speed and force.

An expression of extreme puzzlement crossing her features, Jordon raised her head and stared hypnotized at the round, jagged hole in front of her, directly in line with where her head would have been if she'd been standing straight!

"Dear Lord!" she exclaimed in a dazed undertone. Was that—could that—be a bullet hole?

Suddenly she felt something running down her arm. Blood! she thought immediately. She'd been shot. But when she looked down, fully expecting to see her right arm hanging by a mere thread, she saw instead the squashed carton holding what had been a dozen eggs, a rivulet of brilliant yellow yolk oozing beneath the cuff of her blouse. She dropped what remained of the mess into her basket and quickly scampered a few feet ahead, slipping to her knees behind a large display of English peas and tomato sauce. She wasn't taking any chances. Lately there seemed to be incident after incident of unstable people whipping out guns and shooting people in stores, restaurants, and shopping centers.

Her head swiveled around like the revolving red beam atop a lighthouse as she searched for the gun-wielding maniac and his sawed-off shotgun. It had to be at least something of that caliber, Jordon surmised, her imagination well stimulated by fear, to have made such a large hole in the metal backdrop of the shelves. On the other hand, she thought nervously, she really wouldn't go so far as to classify herself as an expert. The closest she'd ever been to such a firearm was seeing Clint Eastwood or Charles Bronson blasting away with one on TV.

11

What was going on? She groaned as she peered around the cans of peas, her view obscured by several displays similar to the one behind which she was hiding. Darn it! She should have gotten a tissue out of her purse and wiped off her hands. "Great," a tiny voice said, chortling mockingly. *A bunch of criminals are probably waving guns around like the James gang, and you're fretting about a tissue!* Jordon frowned. Was the store being robbed? *Of course it is, you silly goose,* that same annoying voice repeated, jeering right back at her. *Did you think someone was simply strolling through the place, tossing explosive confetti for the sheer hell of it? Oh, sweet heavens! What if they're taking hostages? Who will look after the children?*

"I believe they are robbing the store miss."

Jordon turned and looked at the gray-haired gentleman who had materialized in a crouch beside her, unaware that she'd been whimpering out loud. She looked away embarrassed, vaguely remembering having seen him at the cheese section of the dairy counter as she'd gone by.

"Can you actually see them?" She could barely hear the sound of voices over the hum of the compressors running the refrigerated cases, as well as the music that could be heard night and day. At the moment the store and its occupants were being favored with what sounded like a polka. Jordon gritted her teeth and wished for a pair of earplugs. It was bad enough being caught in such a life-threatening

12

situation, but being forced to endure an unwanted serenade at the same time was too much!

The man stuck his head around the tomato sauce side of the display. After a moment or two he pulled back. "Looks to be some sort of discussion going on up there." He nodded toward the checkout lanes and the high-walled enclosure around the manager's office.

"How many are there? Robbers, I mean?"

"Well," her elderly companion said thoughtfully as he risked another peek, "there appear to be at least three. They have the manager, the bag boy, and three checkers all lying on the floor. Oh, wait," he said quickly, straining to get a better view. "Here comes another one. He's got the butcher. . . . Strange," he muttered after a moment. "They haven't searched the store at all. Apparently they don't even know we're back here."

"Thank goodness. Do you have any suggestions as to what we should do?" Jordon asked, secretly praying for some instant plan that would enable them to escape the frightening setting in which they now found themselves.

"No." The man shook his head slowly. "I can't think of a single thing. I'm afraid I'm not much of a hero. And don't you try to be one, either," he advised. "If they want your jewelry or money, then give it to them."

Jordon looked at him with a mixture of disgust and resignation. She knew that what he was saying was true. But it galled her all the same. Surely there was something somebody could do.

"Uh-oh," her friend muttered as he jerked back behind the safety of the display. "I think we're about to have trou—"

The sound of another gunshot shattered the eerie quietness. This time the bullet slammed into the peas, ricocheted through the tomato paste, and lodged in the end of a shelf a few feet away.

Once those few screaming seconds of unbelievable turmoil settled, Jordon slowly lowered her head. Her dazed eyes saw the most godawful globs of green peas and tomato sauce covering every available inch of her yellow blouse and dark brown skirt. She could feel the same unflattering mixture on her face, on her neck, and in her hair. She turned and stared at her companion just as a lump of peas rolled down her forehead, along the bridge of her nose and dropped with a plop into her lap. The man next to her hadn't fared any better. He looked like some creature out of a science-fiction story.

"Do you suppose they mean to fire in our direction every five minutes or so, or are they such poor shots that they can't control their aim?" she asked with remarkable calm, considering her appearance and the circumstances.

"I wouldn't even hazard a guess," her friend quipped sourly. "Though from the looks of things and the amount of wild gesturing going

14

on up there, I'd say we must have the most incompetent lot of robbers that's ever been."

Jordon frowned. Despite her ignorance where guns were concerned, it was obvious to her that both shots had been fired at random. "I believe you're right. They really don't have any idea at all that we're in the store, do they?"

The man shook his head. "We were both way in the back when they burst in . . . and the only time any of them ventured toward the rear was when one of them went for the butcher. Apparently they've cased the place enough to know that there was a butcher. Though from the way they're acting I doubt it will help them achieve their ultimate goal," he remarked disgustedly.

"So?" Jordon prompted. "Where does that leave us?" She was aware that she sounded impatient, which she was. She was also frightened. She wanted someone to do something. And since the males of the species always seemed to go around with a certain swagger in their walks, a certain something in their bearing that implied "I can do it better than a woman," she secretly wished that her companion would come up with a way to get them the hell out of this mess!

"I think our best bet is to stay here. By the way, my name is Tom Mason."

"Jordon Maxwell. You were saying?"

"Yes, well. Since they obviously aren't aware of our presence, I think it would be best if we kept quiet. Hopefully they'll get the money from the registers and leave. I'll have a perfect description of each of them to give to the police."

"Is that all you can think about at a moment like this, giving the police a description?" she asked incredulously.

"Well, it will be important," Tom Mason retorted petulantly. "After all, if people don't come forward and help the authorities, how can they do their jobs properly?"

"I don't know, and I don't care! At this precise moment my children are at home, waiting for me to fix their dinner. That, Mr. Mason, is what is important to me. To hell with the descriptions of four morons who apparently can't find their way out of this store, much less rob it."

Jordon moved several inches to her right, determined to see for herself what was going on. Finally, by straining her neck like an ostrich, she was able to see the mind-boggling tableau with the four principal players gesturing and waving their arms about. Each one held a pistol that was being carelessly used as a prod when one or the other of them wanted to make a point. Jordon's gaze swung to what little she could see of the "captives" lying on the floor, their arms stretched out in front of them. Some of her annoyance with Tom Mason faded when she saw how erratic the men were acting and how vulnerable their victims were.

"We don't seem to have much of a choice at the moment, do we?" She started to move back to her original position when her knee struck the outside can of peas on the second row from the bottom. Suddenly the tin barricade they'd been hiding behind came tumbling down with a horrendous crash, and Jordon and Tom found themselves looking at the wrong ends of four pistols.

"Christ!" the shortest of the quartet shouted. "What kind of freaked-out pair are you?"

Jordon, once her cover had been blown, sprang to her feet. If she was going to be shot, she'd much rather it be done with her standing than cowering amid a gooey mess of egg, peas, and tomato sauce. "This, my good man," she said crisply, indicating the condition of herself and her companion, "happens to be an example of your generous handiwork. I merely stopped in for a loaf of bread and a quart of milk and a few other groceries. What's your excuse?"

"Whattaya mean?"

For a moment Jordon simply stared at the individual, her eyes running over the less than spanking condition of his clothes and the hole-ridden running shoes he was wearing. She glanced at the others and found them to be in no better shape. What did strike her as odd, however, was the fact that though they were shabbily dressed, none of them looked like they were underfed. In fact, two of them were on the chubby side. At first she'd wanted to believe that they were attempting to rob the

17

store because they were hungry, but it appeared that she was mistaken. From the looks of things they were nothing but common thieves.

"I mean," she began when there was a jerky gesture from an arm holding one of the guns, "what's your excuse for coming in here and harassing innocent people?" The faint sound of a police siren could be heard, and Jordon seized that as extra leverage. "What will you do when the place is surrounded with police?"

"What police?" another of the four piped up, a look of fear suddenly clouding his face.

"The police I hear arriving in the parking lot at this very minute," she said determinedly. "Apparently someone heard those gunshots and called the authorities."

The one that appeared to be the leader of the four turned angrily to the tallest member of the group. "I knew I shouldn't have let you have a gun," he yelled. "Now see what you've done?"

"Well, I only fired it twice," the man said, defending himself. He thrust his chin into the air. "I liked hearing it, Ralph," and then he smiled. "Did you see the way those cans of peas and that tomato stuff exploded? Hell, it looked like Fourth of July fireworks going off. Damnedest thing I ever saw."

"Er . . . what do you plan to do?" Tom Mason asked hesitantly.

"We have to get into the safe in the office," another of the would-be robbers said. He was scowling, his tiny eyes nervously darting about. Jordon was still in a state of shock over how ill-prepared the robbers were. "He says," the man continued, pointing to the manager, who, along with the others, had been ordered to lay on the floor but were now sitting instead, "it's electronically locked till morning."

"I'm sure it is," Tom said hastily and loudly, in order to cover up the groan of exasperation uttered by Jordon. He would have said anything to pacify the four bunglers. "I really don't see anything else for you to do but allow all of us to go free. I'm sure you'll be able to work out something with the police."

"Nothing doing," Ralph said after a thoughtful moment. "We need hostages . . . they're real big in robberies right now. Real big. Hostages and money."

"Don't forget to ask for a plane," another chimed in.

"And hamburgers and hot dogs. I'm not going anywhere without plenty to eat."

"You're joking." Jordan said disbelievingly. Surely she'd heard incorrectly. Four grown men couldn't possibly be that stupid.

"We'll take you." Ralph waved his gun toward the manager and then looked over the rest of his captives, his gaze finally resting on Jordon. "I guess we'll have to make do with you."

"Come on, Ralph. She looks terrible. Her hair is red and green," the tall one complained. "Take that one," he said, nodding toward a

19

cute little dark-haired checker. "She'll be lots more fun."

"We don't have time for fun, Elmer. We've got to think of saving our necks. We're in the big time now," Ralph explained grandly. "There's wheeling and dealing to be done, and from the way she's dressed, she looks like she might be important."

At that moment the sound of an amplified voice could be heard, telling the robbers that the store was surrounded by the police and that they should put down their weapons and come out with their hands over their heads.

"Are we gonna do that, Ralph?"

"Shut up!" Ralph shouted. "I'm thinking, I'm thinking." He whirled around, almost hitting Jordon in the face with the barrel of his gun. He pointed to Tom. "You and you . . . and you," he continued, pushing till everyone but Jordon and the manager were in a line and headed toward the door. He went into great detail to the employees about to be released, relaying the terms by which the hostages would be freed. "And remember," he said threateningly, "if our plan fails, we're going to hold each and every one of you responsible." While the others were on their way out of the store, Ralph hustled Jordon and the manager into the office cubicle.

Jordon looked around, dazed and unable to believe that this was actually happening to her. "Do you feel like you're in the throes of a nightmare?" she asked the manager in a low voice.

"Yes. And what bothers me most is the way they wave those guns around. I honestly don't think they're all that violent. But with the guns they're bombs just waiting to go off. By the way, I'm Seth Bradford. You're Mrs. Maxwell, aren't you?"

"Yes."

"Do you live in the neighborhood?"

Jordon nodded, sensing that the man was attempting to instill a sense of normalcy into the situation by trying to carry on a polite conversation. "On the fringes. I've always enjoyed shopping at your store because you have good meat and your fruits and vegetables are always fresh. Mr. Bradford," she said in a rush of breath, "what do you think they're going to do with us?"

"I wish I knew." He shrugged then grinned. "Are you frightened or mad or both? You came up from behind those peas looking ready to do battle."

"Both, I'm afraid."

For the next four hours Jordon and Seth Bradford sat huddled together on the floor of the office while Ralph perched on the desk. He kept his gun in his hand and the receiver to his ear, constantly talking with the authorities outside. From the amount of arguing going on, Jordon could only conclude that the police were stalling.

She thought of television shows she had

seen where members of special rescue teams burst through walls, the roof, even the floor, to save the hostages. She wished to hell whatever the New Orleans police had that was comparable would get off their duffs and start "materializing," along with their weapons. From that thought, her mind drifted to the two women waiting for her at the shop. "Sorry," she imagined herself saying, "I was detained by four lunatics!"

In the middle of her musings Ralph announced that the police had suddenly agreed to each of his demands. He then went into a huddle with the other three. Jordon and Seth Bradford stared at each other, wondering what was going on.

"Do you think they'll really give those characters a plane and a million dollars?" she whispered in the manager's ear.

"It sure seems doubtful, doesn't it? I don't even know anyone with a million dollars."

I do, Jordon thought, *but I seriously doubt that he'd part with one red cent to save my neck.*

"Keep alert, Mrs. Maxwell," Seth cautioned. "I have this peculiar feeling that once we're out of the store, things will really start to pop."

But Jordon didn't have to be warned. She'd been alert since the first moment the nightmare started. She leaned back against the wall, her arms wrapped around her knees, and closed her eyes, the sound of Ralph and his comrades' voices raised in argument. She wondered if Mrs. Clayton was staying late with the children or if she'd gotten Ellie, Jordon's neighbor, to relieve her? She also wondered if the story was on the news. All the checkers knew her name, since she always paid for her groceries by check. They'd give her name to the authorities, wouldn't they? Lord! The triplets would be terrified if they heard or saw anything about their mother being in danger, especially Amanda. Jordon felt fairly certain that Chad and Jon could take care of themselves in the event that they did hear she was a hostage in a robbery, but her daughter wasn't as rough and rowdy as the boys. She was gentle and quite close to her mother.

Jordon sighed, having no choice in the matter but to believe that Mrs. Clayton or Ellie—or both—were looking after things. She'd learned early on that having triplets had a tendency to turn even the simplest thing into a crisis. Take baby-sitting, for instance, she thought fleetingly. Most of her friends had no trouble at all finding competent sitters, young or old. No one seemed to mind keeping more than one child, as long as they were of different ages. But when they learned that there were three six-year-olds in her brood, Jordon would see the panic in their eyes.

"How on earth do you manage?" she'd been asked dozens of times. And at first, she admitted, she had asked herself that same question. But despite the unholy fear and confusion that had surrounded the birth of her babies, a kind of order and routine had eventually emerged, growing and maturing along with her and the triplets. Jordon was not quite sure of when it was that she had stopped being afraid of the babies. Confidence in handling and caring for them just seemed to be a natural occurrence as the days turned into weeks, the weeks into months, and the months into years.

"All right, let's get moving!" Ralph suddenly burst back into the tiny office, his abrupt entrance startling both his captives. For someone who had been talking almost nonstop on the phone for hours on end, Jordon thought he looked remarkably fresh. Perhaps getting his way had wiped away all the stress. Pity that there hadn't been time for a complete lobotomy, she decided grimly as she followed the store manager out of the office.

"What now?" she asked Ralph as they were joined by the other three. "Do we just walk outside? Are we free?"

"Nothing doing," he countered. "You two are our tickets to a life of luxury. You're coming with us on the plane."

"Where to?" Jordon asked curiously.

"Japan," one of the others sounded off.

"Sweden," another responded.

"I want to go to Mexico," the taller one announced petulantly. "I want to see a bullfight."

Jordon groaned.

"Shut up!" Ralph glared at his entourage. "We're going to Paris, and that's that."

"You didn't say anything about Paris a while

ago," one of the shorter ones said belliger-
ently. "I'm not going. I want my money now."

"Me too," another agreed, jabbing at Ralph
with his gun as if it were a pointer and Ralph's
chest a blackboard.

"We're all going to Paris," Ralph snarled,
waving his gun as well. "It'll take us at least
thirty minutes to divide a million dollars," at
which Jordon and Seth simply stared at each
other. "We'll wait until we get in the plane and
then divvy it up."

"I say no," the short one repeated. He
stepped forward, his gun pointed at Ralph.
"Maybe it's time somebody else made the decisions around here."

"We can't make too many decisions here,
Fred," the more silent one of the four quipped.
"There's a whole bunch of policemen out
there. See 'em?" He nodded toward the glass
front of the store where numerous squad cars
and an ambulance could be seen.

"Do you want to go to Paris, Elmer?" Fred
asked.

"No." Elmer shook his bald head. "I'd
rather stay here and rob stores. This is fun.
'Cept for that man and woman," nodding toward Seth and Jordon. "She looks real messy."

"Shut up!" Ralph yelled again. He reached
out and caught Fred by the front of the shirt
and jerked him forward. "Now get your behind
out that door. We're all going to get on that
plane and go to Paris, France."

Jordon, standing directly behind Ralph,

watched, horrified, as Fred raised his gun. He's going to shoot, she thought when she saw his short, pudgy finger squeeze the trigger. At the same instant there were two loud bursts of noise that threatened to shatter her eardrums. Jordon heard Seth Bradford make a peculiar *whoof*ing noise; in her peripheral vision she saw him slowly falling. But before she could turn to aid him, she felt a stinging sensation against her scalp. And her face was wet, she thought, amazed. It seemed as if someone had suddenly turned on a faucet and was letting a stream of water flow over her head. Even her vision was becoming blurred. She put up a hand to her face and wiped. When she looked at her palm and the tips of her fingers, she saw nothing but red. Lord! How much tomato sauce had she gotten on herself?

The room was taking on a strange swaying motion, Jordon thought as she saw Ralph, El-mer, and Fred staring at her with their mouths hanging open. The taller one, the one who hadn't wanted to keep her as a hostage, was yelling something, but Jordon couldn't hear him. In fact, she thought rather pleasantly, the only sound she could hear was one remarkably like the surf rolling in. How nice, she thought as she floated into oblivion. How very, very nice.

The sound of the front door being slammed brought slender, attractive Lindsey Hines hur-rying from her bedroom toward the spacious living room of the penthouse apartment. On the way she met the stocky, gray-haired W. C., who, for once, lacked the usual calm demeanor that normally controlled his features.

"Do you think he's heard, W. C.?" Lindsey asked, nervously fingering the slim bracelets she wore on her left wrist.

"I doubt it, miss. Earlier, when I called his office, he was unable to be reached by phone. That being the case, I seriously doubt there was an opportunity for him to see the evening news on television."

"Of course." Lindsey sighed, relieved. "Why didn't I think of that? Thank you, W. C., I feel much better."

They entered the living room just as Rand Maxwell was shrugging out of the sheepskin-lined jacket he was wearing along with jeans, a plaid shirt, and boots. He looked tired, Lindsey thought to herself, noticing the fine lines fanning out from the corners of his eyes. His mouth was tight, his lips drawn in a rigid slash. She glanced sideways at W. C.

"I'm afraid we have some rather disturbing news, sir," the Englishman informed his employer. Though he'd been with Rand for nearly twelve years, W. C. staunchly maintained his British reserve, much to the amusement of Rand.

"What's on your mind, W. C.?" Rand asked. He walked over to the tray put out each evening for his use and poured himself a stiff drink of Scotch. As he turned, he tossed the smooth liquid down his throat. "Must be bad." He grinned sardonically at his sister and butler. "Both of you look like you're ready to bolt."

"It's . . . I mean . . . that is—" Lindsey said, stammering.

"The fact is, sir," W. C. said, rushing to the aid of the rattled Lindsey, "your former wife has gotten into something of a scrape, I'm afraid. She was taken hostage in a robbery."

"Good God!" Rand exclaimed scornfully. "I pity the poor bastard that made the unfortunate mistake of taking that shrewish bitch hostage."

"Rand!" Lindsey stared in horror at her brother, disapproval in her blue eyes, which were so like his. "How can you say such awful things about Jordon? From what little I saw of her, I think she was a nice person—a good person."

"Lindsey, my dear, you could find something positive to say about the devil himself. As for Jordon's goodness, I think I'm in a better position to know about that than you. Now"— he looked at W. C.—"why don't you fill me in on the details?"

W. C. did, and as Lindsey watched and listened, she was surprised to see some of the flintiness, some of the iciness, leave Rand's hard features for once.

"Do you mean to tell me she was shot?" he asked incredulously.

"I'm afraid so, sir. She and the store manager, a Mr. Bradford. The police had to storm the market in order to force the ruffians to free Mrs. Maxwell and Mr. Bradford. Seems they— the robbers—were determined to carry their hostages bleeding from the building to the helicopter they thought would be waiting for them."

"Has there been an update on Jordon's condition?" Rand asked, his face looking pinched and grim.

"We've been catching bulletins on the all-news channel for the last couple of hours. I'm sure they'll show all the gory details again, right down to Mrs. Maxwell with her face and clothes covered with blood."

"My God! How bad is she?"

"I took the liberty of calling her home in New Orleans, sir. The hospital has kept the housekeeper, a Mrs. Clayton, nicely informed. The last time I spoke with her, she said Mrs. Maxwell was in rather grave condition due to the tremendous loss of blood. She seems to have suffered a head wound, and there appears to be several bad bruises around her face. We don't know if she was struck by her abductors or what."

Rand looked dazed. For once in his hard-bitten, fiercely fought life he felt as if he'd just been hit in the gut. Damn! There was certainly no love lost between him and Jordon, but the thought of another human being abusing her caused a wave of uncontrolled fury to wash over him.

"Have the children been told?" he asked.

"A very abbreviated story, I believe," W. C. informed him. "The housekeeper and a neighbor, a Miss Eleanor Henson, seem to be taking excellent care of the little tykes."

Rand rose to his feet, his towering height dwarfing his sister and W. C. "You'd better pack me a bag while I grab a shower," he said, nodding to the butler. He turned to Lindsey. "Call Jerome. If the company plane isn't available, then give Lucia a ring and have her make reservations for me on the first available flight. Tourist or first-class . . . it doesn't matter," he threw over his shoulder.

Lindsey watched her powerfully built brother leave the room, then turned to the butler. "You know, W. C., I've got a feeling Rand is more shaken than he's letting us see. And what does he hope to accomplish by flying to New Orleans?"

W. C. was equally perplexed. "Perhaps it's the children," he offered inanely.

"Have you forgotten, W. C., that my brother has steadfastly denied that the triplets are his? He's convinced they belong to Jason Mateo, that old college beau of Jordon's. Rand's supported them, of course, but he's been their father in name only. I don't think he's seen them over a half dozen times since they were born."

W. C. chuckled. "Perhaps he hasn't seen them in person, miss, but their mother has been most diligent in sending him photographs every six months, and all sorts of me-

mentos from the various events in their young lives. It's been most interesting, watching the master's reaction all these years as each package arrived."

"Yes." Lindsey nodded serenely. "Most interesting. I wonder what the outcome of this visit will be?"

"Move it or rent it, sister!"

"Well, really," came the affronted reply.

The slight figure on the bed stirred at the sound of the voices. Someone had told her she was in the hospital, hadn't they? Yes—yes they had, she assured herself. There'd been a . . . Oooh—she wanted to scream in confusion when she failed to remember. What was it they'd said? she thought frantically. She raised a hand to her head. No wonder it felt so peculiar; it was covered with bandages. She bet her hair was a mess. She ran the tip of her pink tongue over the dryness of her lips. Wasn't there any water in this place? Perhaps she'd ask later . . . when they were in a better frame of mind.

She drifted off again, oblivious to the tall, thin, scowling man and the plump nurse who were squared off like two angry terriers.

"You come one step closer and I'll hit you with this bedpan!"

"If you don't put down that damn contraption, I'll throw it and you out that window! I came to see the missus, and that's what I'm gonna do."

"You're not family," the woman tried one last time. "The sign on the door plainly states that only members of Mrs. Maxwell's family are allowed to see her."

"My name's Sid, and that's my boss lady you're taking care of. I've been working for her as a handyman for nearly four years. We trust each other. She gave me a home when I was at my lowest—her and her little kiddies are all the family I got. Now get the hell out of my way, woman. I have to make sure she's all right. You can't believe a damn thing you hear these days. I want to see for myself."

"This is against the rules."

"Woman, if you don't—"

"What seems to be the problem here?"

Both Sid and the nurse whirled around and stared at the tall, powerfully built man with dark blond hair, his blue-eyed gaze shifting back and forth between the angry Sid and the frustrated nurse.

The sound of the familiar, authoritative voice roused Jordon from the confusing haze surrounding her, causing a slight tremor to run through her body.

It couldn't be! It simply couldn't be! a tiny voice began screaming inside her pounding head. Jonathan Randolph Maxwell was in Denver or Texas or Kuwait or wherever the hell his business took him. At least that's where Jordon hoped he was. She certainly didn't want him here. He was a stiff-necked bastard with about as much humor in him as a rattlesnake. On second thought, she decided, perhaps the snake had an edge over him there.

"I don't give a damn if you're the pope, you are not going to bother the missus." Sid glared at Rand. "So what if you're the kiddies' pappy? That don't make you boss in these parts, mister. Jordon might not want to see you."

"Really? Why don't we ask her?"

"Mrs. Maxwell is unconscious, sir." The nurse piped up. "Surely you've heard about the terrible thing that happened to her."

All Jordon caught of this part of the conversation was that something "terrible" had happened to her. With the greatest difficulty she fought against the beckoning mist of unconsciousness. "Will someone please tell me again what terrible thing has happened to me? I can't seem to remember. And what on earth is wrong with my eyes?"

Three faces turned and regarded her with varying degrees of concern.

The nurse, the first to recover from the unexpectedness of hearing Jordon speak, rushed to her patient's side, her manner brisk and professional. "Mrs. Maxwell, how nice to see you awake. I'm Mrs. Withers. I'll be taking care of you at night. Would you care for some water?"

"Please," Jordon murmured. She struggled to open her eyes, wondering why they were so sore. Had she developed some horrible disease that had left her with impaired vision? Was she going blind? Just as she opened her mouth to ask some more questions, the nurse popped a straw between her lips. Jordon sucked greedily, the cool water feeling wonderful to her parched mouth and throat. Her bleary gaze swept the room slowly, then quickly darted back to the man standing directly behind the nurse. Even impaired vision couldn't keep her from recognizing the set of those shoulders or the angle of that arrogant head.

Immediately the water went down the wrong way and she choked.

"Oh, dear." The nurse clucked around like a hen, wiping and smoothing and patting. "Are we all right now?" she asked once Jordon had stopped sputtering.

"No, *we're* certainly not," Jordon snapped. "You haven't answered my question.

"You are in the hospital," Mrs. Withers told her. "You were in a slight accident, but you're doing fine."

Jordon's "Oh" was barely audible, for at that moment she'd successfully focused on the man who was moving closer to the bed.

So it hadn't been her imagination, after all. "What are you doing here, Rand?" she asked ungraciously. "Did they call you and tell you that I'm going to die or something? Are you hoping to put the triplets in an orphanage and forget them?"

A tiny muscle in Rand Maxwell's unyielding jaw twitched in reaction to her hysterical outburst. He stared down at his ex-wife, the dark bruises on her cheek and chin contrasting sharply with the pallor of her skin. Christ! It had been at least three years since he'd last seen Jordon, and then it had been from a distance. She'd looked like a beautiful dark-haired witch, he'd thought at the time. Unfaithful and treacherous as well. At this particular moment, though, she didn't appear threatening in the least. The two bullets that had screamed their way across her skull had left her as pale as a ghost. "You're not going to die, Jordon, and I'm not going to do anything to the children, so stop worrying."

"Then why are you visiting me? We don't even like each other," she threw at him.

Rand looked at the nurse for some indication as to how much he should say regarding the reasons behind Jordon's hospital stay.

"Isn't it nice having company?" the nurse chirped, correctly reading the situation. She slipped a stout arm beneath her patient's head and lifted her so that the pillow could be plumped. "Now, isn't that better?"

"Of course," Jordon murmured vaguely, though she really couldn't tell that much difference. There were so many questions she wanted to ask the nurse, yet she was finding it difficult to concentrate; her head was pounding, and having Rand standing over her wasn't helping in the least.

"You have another visitor." The nurse nodded toward Sid, who moved to the foot of the bed and was stonily regarding Jordon.

"Sid." She smiled weakly at her live-in

handyman. "What on earth are you doing here?"

"Just checking on you. I promised the kids I would see you before I came home. They send their love and"—he reached into the pocket of his jacket and removed an envelope—"this. It's their artwork for today."

The nurse reached for the small package and placed it on Jordon's table. "I'll put it here so that you can look at it later."

"Thank you, Sid. I'm sure I'll be home in a few hours. Tell the children I love them and to mind Mrs. Clayton."

"I will. Now don't you worry. The little ones are fine. Ellie sends her love. She'll be in to see you in the morning. I've got to go." He glared at the nurse. "Take care of her." With a final appraising glance at Rand, he turned on his heel and left the room.

"Rand?" Jordon tried to look around the plump figure of the nurse.

"I'm here, Jordon," he spoke from beside the window. As soon as the nurse moved aside, he walked over to the bed. "Is there anything I can do for you?"

"I don't think so." Jordon frowned. "To be truthful, I can't even remember why I'm here. All I know is that my head is pounding and my eyes are sore."

"I think the soreness that seems to be in your eyes is simply an extension of your headache, Mrs. Maxwell."

"I know I've been told once why I'm here,

but I've forgotten. Would you mind explaining again?" Jordon asked cautiously. "As well as I can remember, this is coming up on the busiest time of the year for my business." She grimaced and closed her eyes. Even talking made her head hurt. "I can't seem to get anything straight in my mind."

"I'm afraid you were in a little accident, dear," the nurse repeated for the second time.

"What kind of accident, Mrs. Withers?" Jordon asked. Had she wrecked her car?

"Why don't we rest now? We'll talk later."

"What kind of accident, Mrs. Withers?" Jordon repeated, becoming more agitated by the second. Having her questions ignored was beginning to make her angry.

"Oh, dear," the nurse murmured. And this time it was she who looked at Rand.

"You had the misfortune to be in a grocery store that was robbed, Jordon," Rand spoke up. "There was some gunfire and you were hit."

Jordon stared at Rand with her mouth open, at the nurse, and then, for the first time in her life, she fainted.

CHAPTER TWO

The next time Jordon awoke, it was dark and very quiet. Only a small night-light was burning in her room, just enough illumination to cast a shadowy glow over everything.

She felt stiff and sore, from the top of her head to the tips of her toes. If only she could stretch. A long, bone-cracking stretch—it would feel so good. She moved first one leg and then the other, and it helped some. But when she tried the same with her arms, she found them hampered by needles and tubes hooked to IV bottles hanging beside her bed.

"Darn!" she muttered, irritated.

"Having problems?"

Jordon turned her head sideways on the pillow, and her gaze encountered Rand's enigmatic one. He was sitting a few feet from the bed in a chair that looked remarkably comfortable for hospital issue, though she doubted that a man of his size would find it so. Rand was six feet—plus several inches. Finding chairs to accommodate his build wasn't easy.

"Rand? What on earth are you still doing here?" He'd left once, right after she'd

38

regained consciousness from having the robbery and the other details told to her for the second time. Why had he come back?

He shrugged as he got to his feet. He walked over and sat on the side of the bed. "I just happened to be in the neighborhood and thought I'd drop by. I told your nurse to take a break, that I'd stay with you for a while."

Jordon knew he wasn't telling the truth. In all his thirty-nine years Rand never "just happened" to do anything. Knowing he'd been watching her as she slept irritated her. Never again would she allow herself to be placed at a disadvantage where Rand Maxwell was concerned. This was the man who had refused to accept his own children and had accused her of having an affair with another man. She didn't feel in the least bit charitable toward him.

"What time is it?" Jordon asked suspiciously. Now that she could see better, she was able to pick up on the subtle changes in his face since she'd last seen him. That had been three years ago. Fortunately for him, she reasoned, the changes time had etched into his face seemed to add something to the overall composite of his features, something that made him more attractive. The added creases at the corners of his eyes enhanced their piercing blue. She could tell that he still fought to control his hair. Though it grew close to his head, it was thick and had a tendency to curl. And, of course, Jonathan Randolph Maxwell was too stern to allow something as frivolous as a wave or the hint of a curl to adorn his obnoxious head. Still, she mused as she stared up at him, she'd always thought Rand to be the sexiest man she'd ever met. Time hadn't changed that, either. It was a shame that she hated him so much.

"It's close to four o'clock in the morning. Can I get you something? Some water? Some ice? Is your headache better?" Rand asked with the proper degree of sympathy that as good as said not to get any ideas, he was concerned about her health, nothing more.

"No thanks. My head is feeling much better. I wish I could stretch, but with all the hardware attached to me I don't think it would be a good idea. Besides, at the moment I'm much more interested in what you're really doing here, Rand."

He continued to stare at her, rather surprised by the changes he was seeing in her from the days when she was his wife. She was mature now, more confident. Missing, he reasoned mockingly, was that quiet air of helplessness of seven years ago that had caused him to make the biggest mistake of his life. That fact had been confirmed when he discovered that Jordon had betrayed him by going to bed with another man. There'd probably been many other affairs since their divorce, he told himself. He'd been lucky to have found out as quickly as he did exactly what sort of woman he'd married.

"W. C. and Lindsey saw the whole thing on

the twenty-four-hour news channel. They saw you and the manager being carried unconscious from the store by the robbers, and the struggle between them and the police to free you. Later in the evening I was able to catch most of it. Pretty gory," he said quietly. "You must have been really frightened."

"Oh, I was," Jordon admitted, "and angry. Those men were so incredibly stupid." She sighed. "I still can't believe they actually got as far as they did. Has anyone checked on Mr. Bradford, the manager?"

"His wife stopped by here earlier and said he was doing fairly well. One of the bullets that hit you ricocheted and hit him in the chest. He was in surgery for several hours while the doctors removed the bullet. As for you, I'm beginning to think you have about as many lives as a cat." Rand grinned. "Are you aware that you were shot twice?"

"No," Jordon said, surprised.

"Both head wounds. That accounts for the ungodly headaches you've been having. One bullet made a nice little trench through the skin and hair on your head, while the other one was a little nastier. That one left you with a slight hairline fracture. According to your doctor, you'll be fine in a few weeks. In the meantime you will have to take it easy and get plenty of rest. You've lost a lot of blood, which will account for you feeling as weak as a kitten."

"When did you find out all of this?"

"I happened to be here when the doctor

made his rounds." There was that word again, Jordon thought. Rand was certainly doing a lot of "just happening" these days.

"And?"

"And?"

"You still haven't told me why you're here. Where are you staying?" Jordon shifted around till she was lying on her side, facing him, not responding when he named a well-known hotel. "Neither of us feel very loving toward the other, so I'm sure it's not a sudden gust of affection for me that prompted your trip to New Orleans."

Rand sat back, his hands locked around one slightly raised knee. He regarded her thoughtfully before answering. "You're right on both counts, you know. There is no love lost between us, but I was concerned for you and for the children. Knowing that you had no family, it just seemed to me to be the decent thing to do . . . for several reasons."

"Well, now that you've done the decent thing," Jordon said acidly, "when will you be returning to Denver?" She sounded like a bitch, but at the moment she didn't care. She wasn't finding it easy being nice to a man who considered her a tramp.

There was nothing in her heart for Rand Maxwell but the deep, never-ceasing desire for revenge. This man, sitting so casually on the edge of her bed, had believed her to be unfaithful to him during their brief, unhappy marriage.

His ugly accusations had hurt her as much as a physical blow. She'd also felt guilty for even marrying Rand, a fact that surfaced only a few months after the ceremony. She honestly believed at that time that she'd used him. But her father's death had thrown a pampered and spoiled Jordan into a tailspin. Knowing that Rand and her father had been close friends caused Jordan to look upon Rand as some sort of surrogate parent. And, she thought as she watched him, she might even have come to love him if his jealousy hadn't been so intense. Consequently any feeling between them, as well as their sex life, became almost nonexistent. Amid the endless quarrels that filled their short time together, Jordan had sought the companionship of her former fiancé, Jason Mateo. When Rand learned that she was still friendly with Jason, he'd immediately jumped to the conclusion that they were sleeping together. A conviction he believed in so strongly, he was never able to hear Jordan's words of denial.

She and Jason had been friends, nothing more, though at the time she'd been unable to convince Rand of that fact. And the more difficult Rand became, the more Jordon turned to Jason. She'd been desperate for a shoulder to cry on, and Jason's quiet, easygoing manner was in direct contrast to that of her jealous, intimidating husband. Rand ranted and raved; Jason discussed things in a calm manner. Rand demanded she give up her friends, quit college, and devote her time to him; Jason encouraged her to continue her education and pursue a career in telecommunications.

"Oh, I'm in no hurry to get back to Denver," Rand drawled mockingly.

"Well, for the life of me I can't see why not." Jordon frowned petulantly. This was the first time since their divorce that they'd done less than go for the jugular vein with each other verbally. She knew she would never forgive him for believing he wasn't the father of the triplets. Nor would she ever forget poor Jason's face when she informed him that Rand had pinpointed him as the father.

"Then perhaps it would help if I apprised you of at least two very excellent reasons. First of all, some "resourceful"—and I use the term loosely—reporter has managed to stumble upon the fact that you are my former wife. It was mentioned briefly last night on the late news, but considering who I am and the fact that I'm not exactly a pauper, I've no doubt the morning papers will be running a lengthy account. More than likely there'll be reporters and photographers hounding you and the children until something else happens to take their minds off this latest story. Since you're in no condition to field the questions, I think it's best if I hang around for a few days. The second thing that occurred to me was that with all the publicity, some nut may think of cashing in on a good thing by possibly trying to abduct you again, or one of the children. Money has a way of making people do strange things, and once the fact that you're my ex-wife—not to mention the fact that you're in a weakened condition—becomes public, someone might decide to make use of it. Aside from those two 'insignificant' reasons"—he grinned mockingly—"I think it's time I got to know *my* children. Don't you?" He was taking unfair advantage, and he knew it. But, he reasoned, he knew Jordon well enough to know that she would waste little time in getting her revenge.

"No, I certainly do not," Jordon snapped. "They've managed quite nicely for six years with only an occasional visit from you. The last one was . . . three years ago? Anyway, after all this time, why would you want to 'get to know' three children that you've said repeatedly aren't yours? Frankly"—she looked him square in the eye—"they hardly know you exist." It was a dirty jab, but he deserved it, she thought maliciously. His apparent softening toward the children should be tickling her to death. On the other hand, she thought drowsily, he had no business upsetting her with all his talk about someone kidnapping them.

"Tsk, tsk. How remiss of you not to keep me always fresh in their memory," he replied innocently. "As to who the real father is, perhaps I'm mellowing. Could be I'm willing to accept what you've tried so hard to convince me of for years . . . fatherhood? Age does that to a person, you know. It might be nice having them around now that they're over the more difficult

45

stage." As he spoke, he all but laughed at the outright fury he saw gathering in Jordon's stormy eyes. "There is one thing that puzzles me, though," he added, frowning.

"Oh? Only one?" Jordon asked, pretending to stifle a huge yawn.

"If you're so indifferent now regarding my relationship with the triplets, why have you been so diligent in sending me a package every six months since they were born, full of details of their almost daily progress and hundreds of pictures? I'm sure the photographer you use is a wealthy man by now, considering the number of sessions you've had with him."

"Why, that's simple, Rand, darling. I wanted to annoy the living hell out of you," Jordon cooed sweetly, disregarding the crack about the photographer. "Have I been successful?"

"Like a toothache," Rand remarked sourly.

"How nice." She switched positions from her side to her back, becoming extremely tired all of a sudden. She'd forgotten how exhausting verbal fencing with Rand could be. She'd had enough. "If you don't mind, I think I'm ready to go back to sleep." She continued to regard her ex-husband. "I do hope you cope satisfactorily with the reporters you think are going to suddenly appear on my doorstep, Rand. Quite frankly, I don't think much of the idea. I've never publicized the fact that I was married to you. On the other hand, neither have I tried to hide the fact. Why should it make such a big splash now? Our marriage and divorce were rather quiet."

"The small town in Oregon where you and your dad lived wasn't exactly the most coveted spot for reporters." Rand grinned. "The sensationalism of the robbery and the fact that you came close to being killed as well as being held hostage, Jordon, darling, has added a dimension of interest in you not present before. You're somewhat of a hero," he drawled with saccharine sweetness.

"Oh." She sighed indifferently, though inwardly she was seething. Damn him! She wanted him to spend time with the children because he loved them, not out of some sense of protection. A prolonged visit from him at this stage of their lives could do little but confuse them. They had always been told that their father worked overseas, and the three times she'd managed to persuade him to drop by and see them, she'd spent days preparing them for his arrival. Having him suddenly sprung on them wasn't the way it should be happening. "If you insist on staying around for a while, you might give Mrs. Clayton a hand. The kids are involved in a number of activities, and she doesn't drive all that well." Almost before the words were out of her mouth, Jordon felt herself slipping off to sleep.

"Certainly," he murmured resignedly, knowing full well that he'd been beaten at his own game. He'd wanted to irritate her about the children . . . it came under the heading

47

of revenge. She'd fielded his sarcastic remarks beautifully. Okay, he acknowledged silently, she'd won this round. There'll be plenty of others in the days to come.

As Rand continued to sit and watch Jordon he couldn't help but notice how her thick lashes cast tiny crescent shadows on her pale cheeks. She looked exhausted. *Don't be a sucker twice in your life with the same woman,* the saner side of him lectured. *You felt sorry for her seven years ago and look what happened. She'd do the same thing again if given even half a chance.*

And yet, as he watched the gentle rise and fall of her breasts, he realized he really was frightened for her and the children. He figured that he and Jordon must have set some kind of a record for disagreeing, which more than likely would continue in the future. But for the moment there was some inexplicable force within him, reminding him that at one time she had been his wife and that—regardless of the past—the triplets carried his name. Thusly, he concluded, that fact alone gave them the right to his protection.

Actually, Rand thought as he eased to his feet, careful not to awaken Jordon, he really meant what he said earlier about getting to know the children. As he'd watched the development of each child—mainly through the pictures Jordon had seen fit to shower him with, he thought grimly—a nagging sense of doubt had begun to eat at him. He'd found himself beginning to question his original beliefs. Each time he looked at the likenesses of the boys he saw features that pulled at his conscience. Features such as their size—each was big for their age. There were also the square chins, deep blue eyes, and dark blonde hair with a slight curl. His gaze became icy, his features rigid. Must be square chins and curly hair in Mateo's background, he persisted stubbornly.

He stood for a moment, his large hands thrust into the back pockets of his pants, and stared thoughtfully at the sleeping figure on the bed. Had he been wrong?

No. He gave a slight shake of his head. No, he hadn't been wrong; now wasn't the time to falter in his stand. Similarities could be found in any number of things if a person looked long and hard enough. The children belonged to Jason Mateo, and that was that. Even now, seven years after they'd parted, he still remembered how Jordon was constantly running to that damn Mateo. "Jason is kind," she'd said, taunting Rand. "He never yells and storms at me the way you do."

Rand's face remained impassive as the memories swept over him, memories that still brought a bitter taste to his mouth.

A simple blood test would have settled the question regarding the triplets' father. But by then the damage had been done. Rand couldn't stand being in the same room with Jordon, nor she with him. He honestly believed she'd betrayed him, and his pride wouldn't allow him to forget. He didn't need a blood test to prove him right.

He'd been a close friend of Jordon's father, Chad Hunter. Chad was the owner of a small tool company. He really wasn't much of a businessman, Rand remembered fondly, but he had been a genius at coming up with new and innovative ideas, several of which the Maxwell Corporation bought.

When Chad suffered a fatal heart attack, he'd been having dinner with Rand. They'd been working out the kinks of a deal whereby the Maxwell Corporation would buy into Chad's tool company and furnish him with a fully equipped lab, which in turn would halt a probable bankruptcy by Chad and at the same time give him an opportunity to devote more time to his first love—creating new ideas and machinery.

Rand turned from the hospital bed where Jordon was sleeping. He walked over to the window, parted the drapes, and stared down at the street below. What was it about the late Chad Hunter, and now Jordon, that seemed to embroil him in the difficulties of their lives?

He returned to his thoughts of the past. He remembered how he'd thought it his duty to stand by and help a grief-stricken Jordon over the shock of her father's death, considering his friendship with Chad. She'd still been at college, and that look of utter despair etched in her face had bitten through the hard core surrounding Rand's heart.

Knowing the financial shape of the company, Rand was aware that if he didn't go through with the agreement he'd entered into with Chad, Jordon not only would have lost her father, she also would be forced to leave school, creating yet another difficult moment in an already chaotic period of her life. Chad had often talked to Rand about his daughter, his voice full of pride as he'd related how eagerly she was looking forward to working in television someday.

A mocking gleam appeared in Rand's eyes as he gazed into the night. He'd certainly looked after Chad's daughter, hadn't he? He'd felt an overwhelming sense of obligation and had married her within six weeks of her father's death. However, as her grief diminished, so had her attachment to him. Hindsight was always so enlightening, Rand thought bitterly. Though she was a passionate woman, Jordon found herself more in awe of her husband than in love. She'd admitted as much to Rand during one of the many arguments. Her honesty had forced Rand to examine his own actions. What he'd found hadn't pleased him at all. So what if love wasn't the overriding ingredient in a relationship, he'd argued with himself. With his wealth and position they could be happy. Later he'd shaken his head at his inept handling of the entire situation. For the first and only time in his life Rand Maxwell felt like a fool. The harder he tried to make up for the unhappiness she'd suffered, the more withdrawn Jordon had become. When he learned that she was still seeing her former fiancé, Jason Mateo, Rand knew their marriage was over.

He turned from the window and reached for his jacket. He held it by two fingers over one shoulder as he quietly walked back over to the bed and looked down at Jordon. At one time this woman had been his wife. When they'd parted, he'd been surprised at how much he missed her. He still resented her for that, resented her for refusing to die in his thoughts, for the peculiar emptiness in his life at the loss. He'd refused even to consider that such a thing as love for Jordon might possibly have been the reason behind his unhappiness.

Now, in sleep, there was something achingly vulnerable about her, some disturbing aura about her that was steadily encroaching upon his senses and awakening old emotions that were better off forgotten. Rand reached out and gently traced the delicate line of her lips with his thumb, his gaze riveted to the sensuous fullness he'd kissed so many times, his features immobile. His thoughts were in turmoil as that quiet touch brought back memories of other times when he'd held her in his arms . . . of times when he'd made love to her.

Suddenly Rand wheeled about and strode from the room, damning himself for his weakness and vowing not to be made a fool of again.

* * *

In spite of a steady stream of company, the next couple of days passed with agonizing slowness for Jordon. Rand was in and out, glaring like some ill-tempered fiend at the different male friends who came to visit Jordon.

"No wonder you divorced him," Cody Grimes murmured on one occasion as he watched Rand stride from the room. "His glance can freeze a person at fifty feet."

Jordon laughed, even though it made her head ache to do so. "He isn't all that bad," she said, wondering why she was defending Rand. But for some particular reason it simply didn't set well to hear him criticized. "He's a very powerful man. I'm sure he's not finding it very pleasant not having a million things to do."

Hank Clark and Tray Gentry, two other men Jordon also dated, were equally awestruck, though whatever their opinions were of Rand, they kept them to themselves. What struck Jordon as comical was the suspicion she saw in Rand's eyes each time a new man showed his face in her room. She could just see his pea-sized brain imagining her in all sorts of illicit affairs.

Jordon hoped the thoughts were driving him crazy. He deserved no peace at all for being such a narrow-minded jackass. Even the flowers that had been sent to her seemed to annoy him. She got the distinct impression that Rand would like nothing better than to throw the lot of them out the window.

On the morning of the fourth day her doctor informed her that she could go home the next day if there was no recurrence of the temperature she'd run the first two days. Jordon was so elated by the news, she practically wrung off the poor man's hand.

"Oh, that's wonderful!" she exclaimed. "No offense, you understand, but this hospital is the pits. I also miss my children."

The doctor smiled. "I have kids of my own, and believe it or not, I *do* know what you mean." He turned to go, then paused. "When you do get home, Mrs. Maxwell, be sure to take it easy for the next couple of weeks. Your body still hasn't recovered from the shock it received. Will there be someone at home to help you?"

"I have an excellent housekeeper."

"Good. I'll see you in the morning."

Jordon laid back against her pillow, smiling for one of the few times since the accident. Tomorrow. She could go home tomorrow. She turned on her side and reached for the telephone just as the door to her room opened and Eleanor Henson, her closest friend and neighbor breezed in. Ellie was a model, and Jordon was accustomed to seeing her in makeup and outrageous outfits.

"Wow!" Jordon gave a low whistle, a saucy grin on her face as she got the full benefit of her visitor, dressed to the teeth in a sheer black cocktail dress over a satin underskirt. A rhinestone clip, a tiny, gauzy arrangement of tulle, and a pink satin rose provided the excuse for a hat, worn low over one eye, that looked incredibly sexy on Ellie. "A little much for this time of the morning, isn't it? Are you on your way home from a wild and exciting evening or on your way out for . . . whatever?" she said, grinning.

"Get your mind out of the gutter, child." Ellie chuckled. She walked smoothly across the room and sat on the edge of the bed, not a hair out of place and her makeup perfect. Jordon felt like a complete dud with her turban of bandages and her multicolored face. "I'll have you know, we're shooting only a block from here in the fabulous gardens of that new bank building. A new wine account." She wrinkled her nose. "My 'exciting evening' consisted of fixing dinner for your children. And I don't mind telling you, the experience probably has put me off having kids forever."

"Were they really terrible?" Jordon laughed. Ellie in the role of surrogate mother was comical. She'd learned that with three of the same age there was a tendency at times for the combination of their ideas to slightly overload their ability to reason. "Where was Mrs. Clayton? She's so good with them."

"Mrs. Clayton, er . . . yes. She wasn't feeling too well, so I told her to go on home. Now don't start worrying about your chickens, honey. Other than a few bumps and bruises on their ornery little heads, they're fine. After their handsome father showed up, I wasn't sorry at all that I'd sent poor Mrs. Clayton home early."

Jordon's attention narrowed, her brown eyes alert. "How often has Rand been to the house?"

"At least twice a day," Ellie answered casually, not missing the surge of color that stained her friend's cheeks. Very interesting, she mused. Jordon became prickly at the mention of her former husband's name, and Rand resembled a porcupine at the slightest reference to Jordon. Interesting indeed. "For a man who hasn't been around them very often, he has remarkable patience with the kids. Before they went to bed last night, he was down in the middle of your living-room floor with both boys on top of him. He doesn't seem at all as you described him," she tacked on innocently.

So Rand was getting to know the children, hmm? After all her efforts of sending every little scrap of information to him regarding their progress and almost hounding him to death, he finally seemed to be thawing toward them. "How did Amanda accept him?"

"Cautiously," Ellie said gently, a little ashamed of her teasing. But Jordon had a tendency to put her head in the sand when there was something in her midst that she didn't want to see.

Ellie knew the story of Jordon's marriage and sympathized. But she also knew, from the past few days of seeing and being around Rand

Maxwell, that he wasn't going to be as easily managed as the other men in Jordon's life.

"Your daughter isn't as readily won over as your sons. They, on the other hand, are beginning to really enjoy their father. They need a man, Jordon. More precisely, they need a father."

"You need not belabor the point, Eleanor," Jordon snapped. "I've been hearing that same line for years. And in case you haven't noticed, I am presently seeing at least four men I consider fairly good husband material. I'll be making up my mind before the year's up."

"How nice," Ellie quipped. "Sounds like you're debating on which car to buy." She glanced at the number of flower arrangements in the room, from red and yellow roses to exotic lilies. "You might start by trying to judge who spent the most on flowers."

"How tacky."

"True. But practical."

"I'm going home tomorrow, isn't that wonderful?" Though the subject of Rand was far from being settled, both knew it was prudent to let it drop for the moment.

"Fantastic." Ellie grinned and meant it. She was quite close to Jordon and the triplets. Learning of the robbery had nearly frightened Ellie to death. "I'll make you a huge chocolate cake. Now"—she rose to her full five feet nine —"I've got to scoot. The life of a model is hell." She leaned down and dropped a kiss on

Jordon's forehead, then was gone, leaving a trail of her own special fragrance behind.

When the door closed, Jordon stared thoughtfully at the ceiling. So Rand really was getting to know the children. Had she accomplished what she'd been striving toward for six long years? Had he finally accepted the children as his? She doubted it. Though, for their sakes, she hoped he would be a little more attentive. As for her, she wanted nothing from Rand . . . nothing at all.

CHAPTER THREE

On the morning the doctor had promised to dismiss her from the hospital, Jordon awoke a little after five o'clock. She threw back the sheet and light blanket, eased shaky legs to the floor, and walked over to the metal sink to wash her face and brush her teeth. "Lord!" she exclaimed after getting a look at herself. She shook her head as she wet a towel. "I look like I collided with a freight train."

The bruises on her face, where she'd hit her head when she'd fallen, had turned a sickly purple. One eye sported a perfect shiner, which she couldn't begin to account for, and the only redeeming feature she could find was that the original turban of bandages on her head had been reduced to a mere two large Band-Aids along her hairline above her left eyebrow. "At least I don't look like I'm wearing a freaked-out hat," she muttered, bending over to splash additional cool water onto her face.

"There's a lot to be said for freaked-out hats?" said an amused voice from the door.

Jordon groped for a towel, wiped her face,

then turned around and stared at Rand. He was standing just inside her room, looking as fresh as a daisy in spite of the early hour. He was dressed in dark gray slacks, a lighter gray pullover, and a navy blazer and was boldly undressing her with those lazy blue eyes Jordon knew she could never forget. He looked tall and big and muscular, and there wasn't an ounce of fat on him. "What are you doing here so early?" she asked.

He made her nervous. She was clad in a pair of light blue pajamas and was perfectly covered. But to be caught in them by Rand made her feel as if she had nothing on but the sheerest nightgown.

"Aren't you supposed to go home this morning?" He walked toward her and leaned against the wall near the sink. "Didn't the doctor say you could go home?"

"Yes . . . yes, he did," Jordon said, nodding. The fresh, clean scent of his after-shave was all around her, making her dizzy with the evocative thoughts it was arousing. Jordon wondered why his nearness should affect her in such a way. This was the man she hated. All she wanted from him was an acknowledgment that he was the father of the triplets . . . which he was.

As close as he was at the moment, she could see the tiny dark flecks in his eyes and the way his thick brows curled a little like his hair. Her eyes became fastened on his chin, a chin she saw every day in both her sons. She wondered if Rand had picked up on the similarity as well.

"Then I offer my humble self as your chauffeur." He smiled. "As soon as you're ready, we'll get going."

"But the business office won't be open till eight," Jordon told him. "Apparently it's been a long time since you were in a hospital. Nobody but nobody leaves until they've made satisfactory arrangements for their bill."

"Not to worry," Rand replied smoothly. "I've taken care of everything."

Jordon pursed her lips and tipped her head forward. "I see. Money does talk, doesn't it?"

Rand shrugged. "Unfortunate but true. Would it make you feel better if I were poor and you were forced to wait till eight?"

"Even I know when *not* to look a gift horse in the mouth," she admitted. "However, my insurance will cover any money you've paid the hospital. But I am curious as to why you came this early. What if I'd still been sleeping?"

"I wanted to avoid the reporters who've been watching the front entrance of the hospital ever since you became a patient here. As for waking you up"—he grinned—"why, I could have pretended you were a modern-day Cinderella and kissed you, or I could have doused you with cold water." He leaned forward from the waist, his face uncomfortably close. "Which would you have preferred, Jordon, mmmm?"

"Well," she said thoughtfully, assuming a

posture of profound thoughtfulness. "I really can't remember what your kisses were like, Rand. That being the case, I suppose I'd have to say the water." She turned away, but not before she caught a glimpse of the wicked gleam in his narrowed gaze and the amused smirk on his lips. Without further pause to savor her small victory, Jordon moved as quickly as her weak legs would allow her toward the bathroom to dress. She closed the door behind her and then leaned breathlessly against it. Crossing swords with Rand at any time was a dangerous challenge, but to do so when one was at their weakest was foolhardy, she told herself.

By the time she'd slipped into fresh underwear, then pulled on a bulky red sweater and a pair of black slacks, a thin film of perspiration had broken out across her brow, and her hands were trembling. She leaned against the wall, willing the weakness to pass. She was fine, she kept repeating to herself, just fine. She had to be. It had been five days since she'd seen the children or been to her office. Five days during which she was positive her business had gone to hell in a handcart.

Jordon closed her eyes against the wavy mist passing before her eyes. It was imperative that she get back to work. Though Rand denied— to her—that the children were his, the triplets were very nicely supported by him. But she took no money for herself. A weak, somewhat wry grin fluttered across her lips as she remembered how shocked the Maxwell attorney had been when she'd refused alimony.

"But that's unheard of!" the tall, angular man—the epitome of corporate law—had exclaimed. "Mr. Maxwell won't like this at all," he'd said with a shake of his graying head. "Won't like it at all."

"Believe it or not," Jordon had said, leaning forward in her chair, "I'm not the least bit interested in whether or not Mr. Maxwell likes it. Frankly I can't think of a single thing I've done from the moment we married that pleased him. Why should I ruin a perfect record at this stage of the game?"

Now, at this precise moment—but only for a moment—Jordon could have kicked herself for her impetuosity. Who knows? she thought grimly. It might be nice to be able to afford to go away for several weeks of vacation till she was stronger. She opened her eyes, thankful that the room had righted itself. But as she stooped over to pick up her pajama top, which had fallen to the floor, she was again struck by the same shimmery feeling of weakness. "Oh," she said with a groan, reaching out and bracing her hands against the tiled walls.

Suddenly she heard the bathroom door being jerked open and felt a blessed coolness flooding over her. "Jordon?" Rand asked sharply, moving to her side in one long stride. Without a moment's hesitation he bent and scooped her up in his arms and strode back to the bed.

"Why the hell didn't you call me?" he demanded in a quiet, furious voice as he laid her down. One large hand clamped itself to her forehead before she had time to try to blot away the perspiration. "You feel as clammy as hell. I'm calling the doctor," he said decisively, turning and reaching for the phone.

Whether the increased acceleration of her heartbeat came from being carried in Rand's arms, or the fact that she was terrified that something was going to keep her from going home, she wasn't sure. But whatever the reason, it lent an added impetus to Jordon's determination to, as of this day, become a "former" patient of the hospital. She jackknifed into a sitting position in spite of the dizziness at the sudden movement, her small hands reaching out and wrenching the receiver from Rand's grasp and dropping it back into its cradle.

"Don't be a complete ass!" she quite nearly yelled at him.

"What's that supposed to mean?" he shot back. "You're as white as a ghost, you're perspiring like a waterfall, and you damn near fainted. Please explain how acting on these three facts make me an ass."

Jordon glowered at him, her lips set in a rigid line, a furious scowl on her face. "I'm going home today, Mr. Maxwell, and I don't need you screwing up my plans. If you do, I swear I will personally cut your throat."

Rand chuckled, his expression far less fierce than it had been only moments ago. "I'm beginning to understand," he said. He sat on the edge of the bed and laced his fingers around one drawn-up knee. "But has it occurred to you that you really aren't strong enough to leave here yet?"

"I must leave here," Jordon insisted stubbornly. "I have a business that will fall apart without me there to look after it. My service is unique, and my clients expect me to be there when they feel the urge to spend money."

"Hire somebody to fill in for you till you're on your feet again," Rand suggested.

"Oooh!" She closed her eyes and looked away in exasperation. "Don't you understand? I *am* my business. It's *me* the customers want to see, not someone I've hired to fill in for me. I have three girls working for me, but I prefer to screen each new account before I accept it. I certainly can't do that if I'm stuck here in this bed for no telling how long."

"Is it really that important to you?"

"Important?" Jordon asked in a disbelieving voice. "That's how I make my living, for Pete's sake."

"Don't you think you sound a little bit foolish, considering my wealth?" Rand reminded her.

"Not in the least. I accepted help from you as long as I was pregnant and until I got on my feet. But when we divorced, I refused any sort of income from you, and I still feel that way. I'm perfectly capable of making my living."

"It wouldn't be forever," Rand remarked

crisply. "I'm more than willing to give you enough money to tide you over this rough spot."

"No thank you."

"You can't go back to work for several days at least."

"I won't know that until I try."

"The doctor said unequivocally that you aren't even to think of returning to work for at least two weeks."

"What the doctor doesn't know won't hurt him."

Rand regarded her through half closed lids for a few moments, then stood. "We'll see. I think we should get packed and be on our way." He got out the suitcase and began filling it.

Jordon watched from the bed, not terribly pleased that he'd given up the fight all of a sudden. "What does 'we'll see' mean?"

"It means, my dear Jordon, that you'd better start trying to figure out a way of gracefully accepting my help, because you damn sure aren't going back to that office until the doctor says it's okay. Now"—he looked around and smiled as he indifferently tossed several pairs of her lacy panties into the case—"have I forgotten anything?"

The trip home left Jordon feeling as limp as a noodle. It didn't occur to her until after she was situated in her home and her own bed, but she was glad that Rand had been there to help

66

her at the hospital; otherwise, she probably would have fallen on her keester. Without the slightest encouragement from Rand or Sid, she promptly fell asleep.

Jordon was awakened from a refreshing nap by a muffled noise outside her bedroom door, closely followed by an irritated "Damn!"

Seconds later Rand entered the room, a tray in his hands. "How does a real cup of coffee sound to you?" He flicked the covers straight with the twist of one tanned wrist and then set the tray across her thighs. "The more flamboyant floral offering is from those three hooligans you call your children," he said with a perfectly straight face. "I'm afraid their efforts put my lowly yellow rose to shame."

Her fingers gently caressed the velvety softness of the single bloom. It was lovely. Yet Jordon had to laugh at the bedraggled bouquet crammed into a squat glass, made up from several of her flower arrangements she'd brought home from the hospital.

"It has . . . character, doesn't it?"

"To say the least." Rand sighed. He started to say something else when a small, dark-haired girl peeked around the door. "Your mother's awake, Mandy," he said gently, holding out one large hand to the child.

Amanda Jordon Maxwell, built on the same diminutive scale as her mother, scampered forward and climbed into Rand's lap, a wealth of questions in her large, dark eyes as she stared at Jordon—especially the huge Band-Aids on her forehead.

"I love the flowers, Amanda." Jordon smiled, anxious to reassure the little girl. "In a day or two you and I will bake some cookies. Would you like that?"

A huge grin spread across the small, freckled face. "Can Ahab help us?" Mandy dearly loved the huge black, tan, and white hound dog named Ahab, who had been rescued from the Animal Shelter four years ago.

"Oh, I'm sure we can work out something," Jordon replied, hedging. "In the meantime I think I need a huge hug and kiss from a certain little girl I know. It would probably cure my headache."

Immediately Amanda left Rand's lap and worked her way around the tray and into her mother's arms. "Now I know I'll be able to make those cookies tomorrow." Jordon smiled after a half dozen or so loud smacking kisses landed on her cheeks and forehead. She brushed back Amanda's hair from her face with a gentle hand. "You'd better go eat breakfast, honey. It'll be time to leave for school in a few minutes."

"Okay, Mommy," Amanda said happily, and ran out of the room.

Rand watched her go, a thoughtful gleam in his eyes. He turned back to Jordon. "The difference between her and the boys is remarkable, isn't it?"

"Yes," she said soberly, "it is. I've often

thought how much Amanda and her quiet gentleness reminds me of your sister, Lindsey."

Rand held her gaze, his strong, white teeth teasing one corner of his bottom lip. "Still trying, aren't you?"

"Of course," Jordon said far more flippantly than she was feeling. "What have I got to lose? You already support them, legally you're their father . . ." She shrugged. "I mean . . . it's not as though I'm asking you to admit to trying to overthrow your government or something. I'm simply asking you to look, really look, at Jonathan and Chad. If those faces and those chins don't convince you, then you're as blind as ten bats and don't deserve to be with them . . . ever."

"I've looked at those faces and those chins, dammit!" Rand jerked to his feet, his sudden movement almost upsetting the cup of coffee into Jordon's lap. He glared down at her, his face a heavy mask of anger. "I don't need you continually nagging me. For that matter, they seem happy enough with our relationship the way it is. You appear to be the only one constantly harping on this acceptance thing."

"What a cop-out," Jordon said disgustedly. "They're only six-year-old children, for heaven's sake. Unfortunately they haven't had to learn about the total asses that account for a large portion of the population of the world. They've always had a picture of you in their rooms, and they accept you as their father . . . it's as simple as that. Won't they be surprised when they learn what you really think of them?"

"What the hell's that supposed to mean?" he asked on an angry breath, his fists clenched, his body leaning toward her.

"Well, surely you can't expect me to keep up this charade forever, can you? It won't be long before the kids will be old enough for me to tell them how you really feel. By then I imagine they will have become attached to their new father, whoever he is, and will eventually forget you. So"—Jordon clasped her hands on the edge of the tray and blandly regarded him—"if I were you, I think I'd go on and leave this morning while they're away at school. And to set your mind at ease, there won't be any more pictures or information sent to you. If I haven't succeeded by this time, then there's no point in continuing to support the photographer, is there?"

Rand took a deep breath, his eyes stormy, his lips tightly pressed together. For one wild moment Jordon was afraid that she'd overplayed her hand, so great was his anger. He looked as if he wanted to strike her. He opened his mouth once, as if to speak, then quickly closed it. Without another word he marched out of the room.

Jordon relaxed against the pillows, a pleased smile on her pale face.

CHAPTER FOUR

"What do you mean, Mrs. Clayton hasn't been here in days?" Jordon regarded Ellie and Rand suspiciously, then grinned rather weakly. "It's a joke." She eased back against the pillow. "You two think you're real cute, don't you?"

"Well . . ." Ellie leered comically at Rand. "He's not exactly what I'd call cute. But if that's the way you see him, then so be it." She let her head drop back and stared at the ceiling. "Mrs. Clayton really hasn't been here since the night of the second day you were in the hospital. Her sister in Mobile is very ill. We have no idea when she'll return."

"Lord!" Jordon exclaimed with a groan, and closed her eyes. "I refuse—positively refuse— even to let myself begin to think of what lies ahead."

"Would one of you mind letting me in on the tragedy?" Rand asked after listening to the conversation for a moment.

"We really shouldn't, you know." Ellie grinned evilly. "We should wait and let you experience the trauma of having sweet-looking little old ladies turn into sharp-tongued

71

witches when they learn about the triplets. Looking for a temporary housekeeper or even a baby-sitter around this place is comparable to the Geneva peace talks. Lots of lip action but very little progress."

Rand looked from Ellie to Jordon, an expression of forbearance on his rugged face. "Surely such a simple matter can't be as complicated as you make it sound." He turned to Jordon. "Do you have any objections to me having a go at it?"

For a moment Jordon was tempted to go into more detail about the problems she'd had getting help. On the other hand, she reasoned, thinking how nice it would be to see Rand bested, why not let the "dear, sweet man" have a go at it—as he'd so aptly put it.

"I think it would be nice of you to take the time to do such a thing, Rand," Jordon said sweetly, so sweetly that her neighbor was finding it difficult not to laugh. "Ellie, will you give him the number of the placement bureau I've used in the past? I believe you'll find it in that little brown book next to the phone in the kitchen."

"Of course," Ellie replied, echoing Jordon's tone of voice. She got up from the side of the bed and headed for the door. "Follow me, oh brave one," she said, motioning to Rand.

Jordon watched them leave the room, a grin of amusement playing about her lips. Rand was a big wheel in the corporate world, she mused. But when it came to finding competent help to manage a house and three lively children, she was afraid that he was in for a big surprise. One part of her wanted him to be successful so that he would get his unwelcome carcass out of her house. But the other part of her wanted him to fail in his mission so that she wouldn't be forced to endure the smirking look of satisfaction she knew would be glued to his face.

She hadn't been home but for a few hours, and already she could tell that Rand was very nicely "running" her household. She didn't like that. Call it jealousy that he could slip in so easily as a figure of authority for the children, or maybe it was just simple pettishness. Either way, it irritated the hell out of her. And Ellie was no help. If Rand were to tell her to stand on her head, Jordon was positive that her neighbor wouldn't hesitate a second before doing as he'd said.

She scooted farther down in the bed, her lids drooping like crazy. It seemed that all she could do was take a nap, she thought fleetingly as she drifted off to sleep.

As she slept, she began to dream. Dreams that were in total conflict with her supposedly rational waking thoughts. In them Rand was everywhere, and Jordon wasn't in the least annoyed by his presence. Quite the contrary, in fact. His arms were around her almost continuously. They went for walks, they talked, and they made love. Made love with such supercharged intensity that a soft whimper could be heard from the quiet figure in the bed.

"I don't believe this!" Rand exclaimed forcefully, startling her from sleep. He'd just burst into Jordon's bedroom and was quite angry. He slammed the classified section of the newspaper down on the bed and glared at her. "Your children, madam, must be carriers of the bubonic plague."

"You mean you weren't successful?" Jordon cooed sweetly, all the while congratulating herself on the wealth of meaning in those five words.

"Don't look so innocent." Rand scowled, his large hands closed into fists and resting on his narrow hips. "You knew I wouldn't find anyone, didn't you?" His dark blue eyes were raking her as if daring her to disagree with him.

"Oh, no," Jordon replied, lying with perfect ease. "You're so forceful, I naturally assumed that there'd be a line of hopeful housekeepers outside the front door within hours."

"Cut the sarcasm," he snapped. He dropped to the edge of the bed and then sprawled backward, his head resting on Jordon's legs. He crossed his arms behind his head and stared at the ceiling. "Why didn't you bother telling me that it would be well nigh impossible to replace Mrs. Clayton . . . even temporarily?"

"Oh . . ." Jordon took a deep breath, hoping to hide the confusion she was feeling at his casual sprawl. In spite of telling herself that she felt nothing for the man, she was finding that being touched by Rand caused her body to respond in a way that wasn't conducive to her peace of mind. "I suppose it has something to do with people like you assuming that if you deem it so, then it surely will be. It's annoying."

Rand turned and stared at her. The nap had done her good, he decided, but she was still too pale, too weak. "Why does it annoy you, and what do you mean, 'people like me'?"

Jordon was silent for a moment as she considered the question. At the moment he certainly wasn't anywhere near as intimidating as he'd been during their arguments when they were married. However, this aggressiveness in him was helping her to better understand why she'd considered him so unapproachable when they were married. Didn't he ever relax? "I don't think I need elaborate on why you annoy me," she said coldly.

Rand frowned. "What are you talking about?"

"I'll tell you exactly what I'm talking about. You're so used to getting your own way. I guess it's only natural for some powerful, wealthy men to think they can make decisions for the entire world."

"Is that what you thought when I asked you to marry me, Jordon? Did you think I was trying to run your life?" he asked stiffly. Damn it! Why had he asked such a stupid question? Rehashing their marriage was something he'd promised himself he'd never do.

"Frankly, Rand, when you proposed, I was in shock over Dad's death. I would have agreed to just about anything. Having lost my mother early on, I grew up with a deep fear of losing Dad. When it actually happened, it seemed like some evil prophecy coming true. As I slowly recovered, I also began to realize how ridiculous I'd acted. You were his friend, and I allowed you to control my life. That was a mistake, and in the end I was forced to assert myself."

"Assert yourself?" Rand's eyes narrowed into icy slits. "Is that what you call sleeping with Jason Mateo?" His angry gaze held hers, damning her for what he thought she'd done and for her daring to disagree with his opinion. Even after this length of time the thought of her in another man's arms cut through him like a knife.

Jordon had thought she was ready to cope with his condemnation of her. During the last few days in the hospital she'd told herself that she'd come to terms with Rand and his hostile feelings. It would be no problem; she could handle it for the short time they would be around each other. But what she saw in his eyes wasn't something that could be healed in a few days' time. It gave her an uneasy feeling.

"No," she began calmly. "I call it confiding in a friend. I'd been engaged to Jason, Rand. It's true that we called off the engagement, but we remained friends. That was the nice thing about our relationship that enabled me to go to him. He was the one person I knew I could trust. He wanted nothing from me but my friendship, and I felt the same way about him. I'm sorry you could never accept that."

"That's your story," he replied cooly. "Frankly I could never understand what kind of problems you had—or imagined you had—that would have caused you to discuss them with an outsider. Why didn't you try talking to me?" he asked accusingly.

"That's a good question. And I suppose about the only answer I can give you is that at that time I was terrified of you. No," she said after a moment's thought, "perhaps awe is a better word. You should be able to understand that, Rand," she inserted with a touch of impatience in her voice. "I was a sophomore in college, rather spoiled by a doting parent, and not even remotely interested in marriage. If you recall, that's the main reason Jason and I called off our engagement. He'd been pressing me to name a date and I balked." She smiled at him, and Rand felt his resolve not to believe her beginning to crumble. "To suddenly find myself married to one of my father's friends—albeit a young friend—was almost as traumatic as Dad's death."

"I did promise Chad I'd look after you," Rand said, feeling the need to remind her.

"I know." Jordon nodded. "And you did so, very nicely."

"Apparently it wasn't nice enough," Rand

said curtly. "We were filing for a divorce before the ink was dry on our marriage license."

"It was a marriage that never should have taken place," Jordon said quietly. "You weren't in love with me, nor I with you. Sexually attracted . . . yes. But even that lost its appeal after the nonstop argument that lasted for the duration of our marriage. We killed all feeling for each other."

"Speak for yourself," Rand told her in a silky voice, his eyes forcing hers to meet his. "Regardless of how angry we got, I always enjoyed making love to you. You were an incredibly sexy lady then, and the intervening years haven't changed that in the slightest."

Jordon quickly looked down at her hands, then at the ceiling, then at the walls . . . anyplace other than back into those dark, hypnotic pools staring so relentlessly at her. This was getting out of hand, she told herself. She much preferred thinking of Rand as her enemy. He seemed much easier to handle that way.

"Er . . . were you able to set up any interviews for a temporary housekeeper?" she asked in a small voice.

Rand laughed. "Tsk, tsk. You are such a coward, Jordon dear." He pushed himself to a sitting position on the edge of the bed, then raised his long, muscled arms over his head and stretched. He looked around at her, his lips drawn in a rueful slant. "You know perfectly well that I wasn't in the least successful."

"Oh, dear," she murmured, her brow creasing. "That is bad." In her mind's eye she saw herself having to endure Rand's help till she was completely recovered.

"Weren't you hoping I'd fail?" Rand asked, thinking how attractive she looked in her own peach-colored pajamas rather than the shapeless hospital gown. He chuckled when his question brought a guilty profusion of pink to her cheeks.

Jordon grinned in spite of herself. "I wonder why my small victory doesn't please me more?"

"Probably because you're thinking of the ungodly uproar there'll be without some sort of help with your three little demons." He waited for Jordon to jump to the triplets' defense and to remind him that the "demons" were his as well, but she did neither. Rand felt somehow cheated.

He reached out and brushed her cheek with the tips of his fingers. The gesture was impulsive, the feel of her soft skin warm and pleasant. "Try to go back to sleep. I'll think of something."

As Jordon stared at him petulantly, her pink lips were full and inviting, awakening in Rand a curious urge to kiss them. "I'm getting tired of those words, you know," she said. "You and Ellie seem to think that all I have to do is flip a switch and whamo! I'm out like a light. I want to get up and move around. I want to do something other than lie here like a hound dog."

"Don't be such a baby," he said huskily. Their gazes met and held. Jordon felt the hair on her arms stand on end. She'd heard him use that same voice with Amanda. It was strong and gentle and indulgent. Jordon had watched it weave its silken web over her daughter and had seen Amanda crawl into Rand's arms, a contented little girl. Now, here she was, feeling that same inexplicable warmth, that same almost irresistible urge to lean on him, that she'd observed in her child.

"You're right," Jordon murmured, "I do need a nap." She quickly turned onto her side, away from him. She was frowning, she was nervous, and she hadn't the slightest idea why. *Don't be silly,* her conscience chided. *You're attracted to the man.*

Once voiced, and though it was only in her mind, Jordon felt as if she'd been kicked in the stomach. She couldn't decide which was worse, her surprise or her disgust. Rand had tried to humiliate her by denying his own children. That act alone was enough to have crushed a lesser person. But she'd made it, Jordon told herself. She made it on her own, and she'd be damned if she would let a few half baked emotions make her forget that Rand Maxwell hated her guts.

After leaving Jordon's room Rand went to the kitchen. He walked over to the wall phone and lifted the receiver. Within seconds W. C.'s perfectly controlled voice was on the line.

After exchanging pleasantries Rand got down to the reason for his call. "How would you like to visit New Orleans, W. C.?"

CHAPTER FIVE

"New Orleans, sir? Why, I think it would be a splendid idea," W. C. replied immediately. "I've read a great deal about their wonderful food. It'll be interesting to see if it's as good as they claim."

"Believe me, it is." Rand sighed. "I feel like I've gained at least ten pounds."

"Oh, dear," W. C. tut-tutted. "That won't do at all. Now, sir," he continued briskly, "why am I needed in New Orleans? Is Mrs. Maxwell worse?"

"Not at all," his boss assured him. "She came home bright and early this morning. The problem is, her housekeeper had to leave suddenly, and we can't find a replacement. I've checked with every available placement bureau and have gotten nowhere. The minute they hear the words *six-year-old triplets*, they almost hang up on me. I'm beginning to think that Mrs. Clayton must be some kind of god or something. Think you can handle the situation until everything's back to normal?"

"Certainly," W. C. answered without the slightest hesitation. "I'll check the airlines and catch the first available flight. Does this mean you'll be coming back to Denver?"

"Er . . . No . . . no. There are a few things I still need to get straight down here," Rand responded in an uncertain tone of voice. Wisely W. C. did not pursue the point. He had his own thoughts regarding the "few things" his employer had to get straight.

By the time Jordon awoke from her nap, she decided it was time for her to get up and move around some. The doctor had assured her that it was fine for her to be up and about, as long as she didn't overdo it.

"Anything is an improvement over this darn bed," she muttered as she swung her feet to the floor. For a moment the world went into a crazy tailspin. Jordon sat very still, not attempting to get up until the dizziness had passed. Once everything was back to normal, she headed for the shower.

Several minutes later she stood before the closet, staring at her clothes, trying to decide on something that was as comfortable as her pajamas but wasn't pajamas. Some order, Jordon decided as she pulled a yellow oxford shirt and a pair of tan slacks from their hangers. The kids needed to get back to normal as quickly as possible, and one of the best ways she could think of to help them do that was to let them see their mother in her usual clothes.

Just as she turned with the clothes in her hands, the door to her bedroom opened and Rand strode in. When he realized that Jordon wasn't in the bed, he came to an abrupt halt in the middle of the room. "What the hell?" he murmured, his head swinging around toward the startled sound that came from Jordon. His lambent gaze was like hot tongues of fire licking at her as it touched on her body, which was bare except for flesh-colored briefs and bra. He felt the rekindling of old desire for her rearing its ugly head deep within him. His hands, at his sides, slowly began to clench into tight, hard fists. What the hell was there about this woman that could turn him on, even when she looked as pale as a ghost, having not a speck of makeup on?

For some crazy reason not a single part of her body, save for her rapidly breathing chest, seemed capable of moving. With a superhuman effort Jordon broke the coursing of excitement arcing between her and Rand. It was stronger than any emotion she'd ever felt, and it left her trembling.

"I'm sorry," Rand said softly, as shaken by the inexplicable electricity pulsing between them as he could see that Jordon was. "I assumed you would still be in bed."

"That's all right," Jordon whispered as she dropped the slacks to the floor. She slipped her arms into the shirt, quickly buttoned it, and then picked up the slacks and stepped into them. "I—I—my back was hurting when I woke up, so I thought it might help if I got up for a while." She turned around and looked in Rand's general direction. Though in actual fact, she told herself, at that particular moment nothing on the face of God's green earth could induce her to look him straight in the eye. She stared at his right shoulder, and hoped that her face did not reveal too much.

"A few minutes on the sofa might not be bad for you," Rand said after a moment's silence. He, too, was having a hard time getting his emotions under control. *Watch it, Maxwell. Don't make a damned fool of yourself again.*

"Don't be such a fussbudget, Rand," Jordon said in an almost normal voice. "I need to start getting up. Besides, I don't want the children seeing me in bed when they come home. At their age they're very impressionable."

"Don't worry, honey," he returned mockingly. "I don't know about Amanda, but I doubt that anything short of dynamite could mess up your sons' psyches. They have hearts and heads as hard as granite."

"Oh, dear." Jordon laughed softly. "Am I to gather from those unkind words that you've locked horns with the boys?"

"No, Mrs. Maxwell," he answered smoothly. "I threatened to tan their behinds or cut off all treats."

"What did they opt for?"

"Having their behinds tanned. Seems they'd endure almost anything rather than give up their food. They eat like two starving bears." He was grumbling, but there was also the light of amusement deep within the dark blue of his eyes.

"And did you spank them?" Jordon asked curiously, not sure how she would react to his answer.

"No, Mother Goose, I did not treat your little ones unkindly," he said, chuckling. "Although," he added soberly, "I wouldn't hesitate to do so if I thought it was necessary."

"There's no point in borrowing trouble, is there?" Jordon said tightly, then turned and walked from the room while Rand stood staring after her, not having the slightest problem imagining her coming after him with a broom if he threatened any of her babies!

Rand hadn't been making idle threats, she kept repeating to herself as she moved about the house, touching and simply looking at her things, and in all fairness, he had a perfect right to discipline his children. Yet Jordon didn't know quite how to handle that aspect of this new relationship. There'd never been anyone else to help her raise the triplets other than Sid and the housekeeper.

But if you are really sincere in what you've been working toward for years, a whispery voice in the back of her mind reminded her, *then you're going to have to accept a number of different things into your life.* Jordon sighed. Rand wasn't a brute. She knew she didn't have to worry about him hurting one of the children. So? The question was short and succinct. So, she told herself, perhaps she was jealous.

Rand found her in the boys' room where she

was idly moving the books around on one shelf.

"What the hell do you think you're doing?" he stormed from the open doorway, his face a mask of fury.

Jordon looked behind her, pretending to be searching for another person in the room. "Were you talking to me?" Christ! The man was like a blinking jailer!

"Who the hell else?"

Jordon clamped a tight lid on her temper. She knew it wouldn't do at all for her to get into an argument with Rand. "I suppose you could say I'm reacquainting myself with my house." She lifted her hands expressively. "It's good to be home. One never truly appreciates a thing until one almost loses it, and all that. Any objections?"

Rand looked kind of sheepish, his anger such a blazing force only minutes ago but now replaced with chagrin. "Sorry," he said with a shrug. "I naturally assumed that you'd decided to do some spring cleaning." He walked over and stood beside her, close enough that their arms brushed. "I've fixed you a snack and a glass of milk."

"I couldn't possibly eat—"

"Don't argue!" Rand said sharply, his enigmatic gaze sending a shiver up her spine as he stared at her. Suddenly he reached out, clasped her shoulders, and turned her to face him. His fingers were biting into her flesh, but for some reason Jordon didn't seem to mind.

"Why do you always argue with me, Jordon?" he asked in a raspy whisper. His hands left her shoulders and began moving lightly over the delicate bones of her neck and shoulders. She was so fragile, he could snap the bones in her body with one hand.

The tips of his fingers were hot, firm points, and they excited her incredibly. The cloth of her shirt provided very little protection against the heat he was generating, and at that precise moment Jordon resented even that small barrier between them.

"It . . . it seems to have become a habit where we're concerned," she offered inanely, unable to tear her eyes away from his mouth, which was moving toward hers slowly. She could feel his hands pulling her closer and closer to the thoroughly masculine length of him, her body relaxing and following the gentle but firm lead without the slightest hesitation.

This shouldn't be happening, Jordon told herself. She'd sworn years ago never again to let Rand Maxwell into her life. What had happened to such a determined promise?

"Have you ever wondered what it would be like for us to be together without some sort of crisis defining the relationship?" Rand asked. His breath smelled of coffee and tobacco, reminding Jordon that he used to overindulge in both.

"No." She smiled softly. "I can't say that I have. Frankly my thoughts where you've been

88

concerned have nothing to do with trying to figure out ways for us to be together."

She heard his deep chuckle the moment his lips touched hers.

Jordon had thought herself a mature woman. She'd dated any number of men in the last few years. And, she reminded herself, hadn't she even pointed out to Ellie a couple of days ago that she was seriously considering which of the men she was presently seeing would make the best husband and father?

But when she opened her mouth to the demanding probe of Rand's tongue, she promptly forgot that those other men even existed, that Rand was the most despicable person on earth, that she'd considered, when she was pregnant, how best to publicly humiliate him, that murdering him had flitted through her mind on more than one occasion. She reeled in shock at the electric surge of excitement that exploded in her when her own tongue caressed the teasing tip of Rand's.

Her knees became rubbery. Her fingers found their way to his strong shoulders, enjoying the feel of muscle and strength beneath her touch, but she also had enough presence of mind to know that she needed something to hold on to, something solid that could support her through the maelstrom of desire springing to life within her. She told herself that she'd made a mistake when she didn't immediately move out of his arms. That became disturbingly obvious when the firmness of his palms sought the tender sides of her breasts, drawing a gasp of pleasure from Jordon.

A sense of reality finally managed to insinuate itself into Rand's brain, reminding him that the woman he was holding in his arms, the woman responding so beautifully to his lovemaking, was the same woman who had been shot only a few days ago. She was recovering from a concussion and was still considered by her doctor to be quite ill. He must be totally without feeling, he realized. But as he brought his hands to Jordon's shoulders and eased her back from him, it occurred to Rand that she looked none the worse for wear. In fact, he quietly mused, there was more color in her cheeks than he'd seen since his arrival in New Orleans.

"I'm sorry, Jordon," he murmured huskily. "Not for kissing you," he clarified, "but for having such lousy timing. I should have waited till you were back on your feet."

Jordon opened her eyes. Her weakened physical condition, plus her highly emotional state at the moment, had left her feeling vague, as if she were floating. However, she thought with a sinking heart, looking into Rand's unreadable eyes made her realize just how ridiculous it really was for her to be standing in his arms. The fact that he had kissed her and that she had responded so readily was something she would deal with later. At the moment she was concerned with salvaging what little remained of her dignity.

"No harm done, Rand," she said smoothly. "I am curious about what you just said, though. What does it matter that you kissed me when you did?" She stepped back a couple of steps, marveling at how in command of her emotions she sounded, when in reality her nerves were as taut as a tightly coiled spring. She deserved an Academy Award.

"You're ill." Rand frowned, baffled that she would even pose such a question. He reached out then, his big hand trembling slightly as he brushed his knuckles against her still pink cheek. He wanted to touch her. He wanted to stop arguing every other breath with her . . . and if he were one hundred percent honest with himself, he quietly admitted, he wanted to make love to her. "But even so, you're still very appealing."

There was a struggle going on inside of Rand, more formidable than any he'd ever faced. He was finding himself having to keep a constant vigil over his emotions. One tiny slip and Jordon would have him wrapped around her little finger. He couldn't allow that to happen, he kept telling himself. But in spite of everything he knew about the woman standing in front of him, his arguments against her were growing weaker and weaker.

Jordon forced herself not to give in to the nervousness threatening to overcome her. She remembered from before how devastating Rand could be in his more amorous moods, she reflected ruefully. He was playing . . .

nothing more. "As I've already said, no harm's been done. Why don't we go check out that snack you fixed for me? I wasn't hungry till you mentioned food. Now I'm starving."

A man accustomed to handling all sorts of delicate problems, Rand revealed nothing of what he was feeling. He agreed with Jordon's suggestion and followed her to the small breakfast area in the kitchen.

"I seem to remember you having a distinct preference for malteds," he remarked as Jordon took a seat at the walnut gateleg table. "It's been awhile," he said softly, almost as though talking to himself, while he poured the mixture into a tall glass and then added a spoon and straw. "However, I don't think I've altogether lost my touch."

As the glass was placed before her Jordon removed the spoon and popped it into her mouth. "Mmmm," she said with a sigh. "Indeed you haven't. This is delicious." She turned and regarded the blender. "Is there enough for seconds?"

"Don't be such a pig, Jordon," Rand said, teasing her. "If you still aren't satisfied when you've finished that one, I'll make you another one." He reached for a yellow legal-size pad. "Since Mrs. Clayton is away for an indefinite period of time and Ellie's work schedule is so erratic, I seem to be elected to do the grocery shopping." He drew a deep breath that clearly bespoke his opinion of such lowly duties but also indicated his willingness to do his part.

92

After jotting down several items he personally remembered they were out of, he looked inquiringly at Jordon, who was sucking so hard on the straw, her cheeks were caving in.

Rand laughed. Funny, he thought, he couldn't remember her being so entertaining when they were married. "You look like an idiot," he said, his voice tender.

"Ahhh." Jordon leaned back and wiped her mouth on the napkin he'd provided. "But a full one." She looked wistfully at the empty glass. "I think I'll forgo the second one till after dinner, though."

"Don't look so sad," he told her as he went back to his grocery list. "I promise not to let anyone steal the blender or the ingredients needed for your pigging-out periods."

"That's unkind." Jordon sniffed haughtily, falling easily into the pleasant ambience that seemed to have evolved of its own accord.

"But true," Rand remarked. He rested one muscled forearm on the edge of the table and stared thoughtfully at her. "Do you feel like taking a look at the pantry and telling me what else I should add to this list?"

"Yes!" Jordon exclaimed, a little too eagerly. She immediately got up and began opening cupboard doors and drawers, working her way to the small cupboard next to the refrigerator. By the time she'd finished, Rand had made one line from top to bottom on the sheet of paper and was beginning the second one. "Are you sure you want to do this?" she asked.

93

"No problem," he replied bravely. Privately he wasn't so sure. He'd never grocery-shopped in his entire life.

Jordon sat back down, a little dismayed to find that that brief amount of exercise had left her trembling. "This is ridiculous," she muttered disgustedly.

"Not really," Rand said soothingly. He'd been watching her out of the corner of his eye and could see a fine line of perspiration on her brow. She was still as weak as a kitten, and the fact that she was so helpless pulled at a sympathetic nature well hidden beneath his usual granitelike veneer. "You're still a long way from being recovered, honey. 'Little ole concussions' take time to heal." He smiled.

"I suppose you're right," she admitted grudgingly. As she let her gaze slide around the room Jordon sighed. The general appearance of the house was beginning to deteriorate. The clutter of three children, plus that many adults, was beginning to show. "If we don't find a housekeeper soon, the health department will force us to move."

"Something will turn up," Rand said soothingly. "Until it does, Sid and Ellie and I will manage."

"Speaking of Sid, where is he?"

"I believe he's finishing up that little job he began for one of your neighbors before your accident. He thinks he'll be through within a week or so. He helps quite a bit around here, doesn't he?"

"Oh, yes." Jordon nodded, her eyes brightening—as Rand had intended—as she briefly forgot her problems. "He keeps the house painted and the yard immaculate. If he hears the tiniest noise in my car, he'll spend all night looking for it."

"How did the two of you get together?" Rand asked curiously. A sort of unspoken truce had cropped up between him and the handyman. They weren't friends; neither were they enemies.

"He did yard work in the neighborhood for two summers. Toward the end of the second summer he became ill. He tried to work, but it was quite obvious that he simply couldn't. When I told him to go home and go to bed, he told me he didn't have a home." Jordon shrugged. "That's when it hit me that I had a place for him. The former owner's hobby had been woodworking, and he'd spent considerable time fixing up the room off the garage. It made a perfect place for Sid. He has his own bath and private entrance. He still does his yard work in the neighborhood during the summer." Jordon grinned.

"I wonder what he was before the handyman segment of his life?" Rand asked curiously. "Beneath that gruff exterior I detect a very sharp mind, and when he occasionally forgets to cover it up, an educated mind. Do you suppose he's ever been in trouble with the law?" Sid's presence had bothered Rand from the beginning, but he hadn't wanted to approach the subject till he felt Jordon was stronger. It wasn't that he disliked the man; it simply boiled down to the fact that Jordon and the children were living alone with an elderly man they knew nothing about.

"I had a friend run a check on him," Jordon admitted. Rand expressed his surprise, and instantly her temper flared. "Did you think I'd take a strange man into my home, especially a home with three small children, and not have him investigated? You must think my brain no bigger than a flea's!"

"Sorry." Rand held up his hands defeatedly. "I apologize. I'm also very proud of you. But then"—he shrugged—"I don't know why I'm so surprised. You've done a remarkable job of building a new life for yourself and the children. Frankly, when we divorced, I didn't know what to expect."

"What you really mean," Jordon said, grimacing, "is that you naturally assumed we would be a millstone around your neck, didn't you?"

"Something like that."

"And when we weren't?"

"I was relieved . . . naturally."

"Were you?"

"Certainly," Rand said gruffly. He pushed back the cuff of his black sweater, then stood. "We might be a little late getting home, so don't worry."

"We?"

"The kids. I'm taking them grocery shopping with me."

"But that's not nec—"

"I think it is," Rand cut in firmly. "There's been two reporters sitting in their cars across the street from this house for two days. The press is having a field day with us. Remember me warning you of something like this happening?"

Jordon nodded, too amazed to speak.

"That's why I'm picking up the children. Sid or I will continue to do so until our 'notoriety' blows over. Okay?"

"Sure," Jordon murmured weakly. What else could she say?

"Come on," Rand said quickly as he pulled her to her feet and turned her toward the bedroom. He didn't like the look of uncertainty in her face. She seemed to find it humiliating to have to accept his help. She was a strong individual. She'd raised her kids alone, and she'd managed to start her own business. Regardless of the conflict between them, he had to admit that that took guts.

Jordon crawled into bed without the slightest argument, lying still while Rand straightened the covers, got her a glass of water, and adjusted the draperies. "Can I see the newspapers?" she asked.

"Why not wait a few more days?" he said easily, his voice belying the hard glint of his blue eyes.

"No, I want to see them now."

Rand frowned, but he turned on his heel and left the room. In minutes he was back with a stack of papers. He dropped them down on the bed. "Don't let all that garbage throw you," he ordered, and Jordon almost smiled at the command.

"Deeming it so again, Rand?" she couldn't help but ask.

Remembering their earlier conversation, he shrugged and murmured, "Old habits die hard." Then he walked to the bedroom door, but before leaving the room, he stopped and turned, his expression enigmatic.

"Where is Jason Mateo?"

CHAPTER SIX

"Wh-what did you say?"

"Where is Jason Mateo?" Rand repeated.

"I haven't the slightest idea. Why?"

"I've been waiting for some mention of him ever since I arrived in New Orleans. So far there's been nothing. You'd think, in view of what's happened, that he would have called or something."

So great was her anger, Jordon thought for a moment that she was going to explode, and for a moment she acted rather than thought. Her hand dropped to the small paperweight that had been a gift from one of the boys. She felt her fingers clutching it tightly in her palm and lifting it. Before Rand could stop her, she raised her arm and hurled the piece of thick glass toward his detestable head. "You are the complete . . . the total bastard!" she yelled at him.

Rand saw the object that was intended to put a large hole in his skull fly toward him and dodged to one side only a mere second before it hit the wall. Somewhat shocked, he stared at the absolutely furious Jordon, who was glaring murderously at him.

"Get out," she demanded in a low, angry voice. "Don't bother going after *my* children, Mr. Maxwell. In fact, don't bother doing another thing in this house. We can take care of ourselves. I despise you. You are lower than a snake's belly, and I loathe you."

"Is that all?" Rand murmured. God! She was angry. He hadn't expected Jason Mateo's name to be mentioned without there being some sort of discussion, but he certainly hadn't expected Jordon to try to part his skull over the matter. Dammit, he was curious about the man. However, if looks could kill, he'd be pushing up daisies this very minute.

Jordon stared at him for a second or two in mute anger, then dropped back against the pillows, one slim hand going to her head, which had started throbbing like crazy. "Please leave," she muttered stubbornly. In her haste to find a weapon suitable for murdering her "darling ex-husband," she'd knocked her pain pills to the floor.

"What's wrong?" Rand asked in a slightly jeering voice. "Has the cat suddenly got your tongue?" He'd been a perfect ass for mentioning Jason Mateo's name, he silently acknowledged, but aside from his natural curiosity regarding the man, he'd begun to feel desperate. The closeness that was suddenly slipping into his and Jordon's midst was frightening. It was like history repeating itself, he thought grimly.

Jordon was in trouble, and he was taking it upon himself to fix everything. Didn't he ever learn?

When there was no response from Jordon, he walked gingerly to the foot of the bed, fully expecting something to be hurled at his body. Her eyes were closed, but there were the telltale traces of moisture inching its way down her cheeks. One hand was pressed to her head, and at that moment Rand felt like kicking himself.

He moved around the bed and sat on the edge. One large hand caught Jordon's and held it; the other slipped beneath her chin, his fingers firm as he urged her to look at him. "I'm not going, you know, till you talk to me." As expected, Jordon immediately regarded him through slitted lids.

"Go to hell!"

"Madam, please," he replied in a comically pious voice. "I'm going with your children to the grocery store."

"Are you inferring that my children are horrid?"

"Yes."

"Then don't bother picking them up, but be sure to do your shopping at Dupree's Family Grocery. Perhaps my robbers have friends who'll be gracious enough to shoot you in the ass!"

Rand placed both palms against his behind in a gesture of imagined pain. "That would be terrible."

"But I'd love every minute of it." Jordon smiled grimly. "I'd come see you every day. I'd laugh at you, and I'd personally bribe the doctors to let me have a picture of your injured tush. I'd have it published in every newspaper and scandal sheet in the country."

"Damn, I only mentioned the miserable bastard's name once," he protested defensively. "How was I to know it would touch off World War Three?"

"I'm serious, Rand. I don't want you here." She started to say something else but didn't. The pain in her head was making it difficult to concentrate on anything, even quarreling with Rand. She inched to the edge of the bed, then began feeling around on the floor with her hand. She had to find that medicine.

"What are you doing?" Rand asked, watching her curious scramblings.

Nothing in the world would have suited her more than telling him to go to hell, but she didn't. "Looking for my medicine," she answered faintly.

"Why didn't you say so, you silly little nut?" In a flash she felt him moving her over in the bed, then heard the rattle of the pills as he found the bottle and opened it. While he watched her swallow the medication with some water, Rand found himself fighting with his conscience. He knew he was the reason she was in pain, and it wasn't sitting well with him. He would exchange insults with her all day long, but doing something to physically hurt her wasn't his style.

"I'm sorry, Jordon," he said quietly once he'd settled her again and saw her drifting off to sleep. He leaned down and brushed his lips against the rapidly throbbing pulse in her temple, cursing himself for not having thought before he'd spoken. When he straightened, the scent of her still clung to him, teasing him, evoking images. Memories pulled at Rand; it was the same perfume he'd given her that first Christmas they'd been together. What the hell did that mean?

You stupid jerk, his conscience jeered, *it means that she liked that particular fragrance. You and the perfume aren't a package, buster, so don't start seeing things that aren't there. Just because you were a blithering ass a moment ago, with a tongue going fifty miles an hour and gaining momentum by the second, doesn't mean your darling ex-wife has suddenly turned into someone different. She's the same woman. The same one whom you have been telling yourself you've hated for the past seven years. The same woman you still halfway think was unfaithful to you. She's still the mother of three children, children you've vehemently denied . . . till these little doubts you've been having lately.*

A deep sigh of frustration escaped his sensuous lips as he contemplated the chaos that had erupted in his life during the last few days. He looked down at Jordon's hand, which he'd absently picked up, and gently stroked her skin with his large palm. It was too pale, he decided.

She should be tanned, and she definitely should weigh more. Even the doctor had told him that Jordon was too thin.

What the hell was he going to do? Or, more appropriately, what did he want to do? Jordon was different from the girl he'd known seven years ago, of that much he was certain. Or was she? Back then he'd really never gotten the chance to know the real Jordon. The marriage had been nothing more than a miserable few months, followed by a hostile divorce and an openly declared war ever since.

Rand's thoughts were heavy as he drove to the school the triplets attended and collected them. The moment the small bodies climbed inside the rental car, however, he had to grin. Their noisy arrival brought with it total bedlam, and Rand immediately found himself thrust into the role of mediator between Jon and Chad. Amanda, he noticed, ignored her brothers' squabbling and sat calmly on her knees in the front seat and stared out the window.

She was so quiet, in fact, that Rand began to worry. He reached out and gently ruffled the soft ringlets on her head. "Something bothering you, sweetheart?" he asked softly.

"Yeah!" Jon leaned eagerly over the back of the front seat. "Mandy's got a boyfriend. Mandy's got a boyfriend," he imparted in singsong fashion.

Amanda suddenly swung around, a sturdy book in her hand, and whacked her brother smack in the middle of the forehead. Rand's "Wait a minute, honey" and Jon's blood-curdling yowl of pain was followed by Amanda's "You hush, Jonathan Hunter Maxwell! I do not have a boyfriend." Her arm was held back threateningly, the book still clutched in her small hand in case he needed further persuasion.

Rand, convinced that there was going to be further confrontation between the two, and afraid that Jon's eye might be hurt the way he was holding his hand over his face, brought the car to a halt as quickly as possible. "Now, kids," he began as he turned in the seat. Unfortunately he found it very difficult to reprimand the furiously frowning little girl standing beside him on the seat. He suppressed a grin, then turned to Jon. "Let me see how bad it is, son." Other than an inch long welt on his forehead, the youngster didn't seem to be the worse for wear.

"Okay," Rand said sternly. "*You*"—he pointed at Jon—"are not to pick at your sister anymore. Understand?" At Jon's hurried nod Rand turned to the still angry minx beside him. "And you," he said in a softer voice, "mustn't be so quick to hit your brothers. If the lick had been a little lower, Jon's eye could have been seriously hurt. Do you understand, Amanda?"

"Yes," she answered. "And if he picks at me again, I *will* hit him in the eye," she said determinedly.

"Hmmm. Well," Rand murmured to no one

in particular, recognizing a Mexican standoff when he saw it. He glanced over his shoulder at Chad, who had remained blissfully uninvolved in the fight. "Er . . . how about helping me keep the peace, hmm?"

"Sure." He grinned and immediately began watching his brother and sister in such a surreptitious manner that he was sure to bring about another war within minutes.

Rand started the car and sped to the grocery store, hoping a change of scenery would bring peace. Good God! How did Jordon cope with all three of them? he wondered hazily as he parked, got them out of the car, grabbed Chad by the collar just in time to keep him from being flattened by a truck, kept Amanda from hitting Jon, and finally managed to get all three of them into the store without a drop of blood having been let.

As soon as he paused for a moment, closing his eyes and thinking how well he was doing, there was a loud crash. Rand opened his eyes. They became rounder as he stared straight ahead at what used to be a display of apple juice that had been toppled by a grocery cart. A grocery cart being yanked around by Chad and Jon.

He vaulted forward with the speed of an Olympian sprinter. "What happened?" he asked in a stunned voice. He grabbed each boy by the arm and yanked one to each side of him. "What started it this time?" he demanded.

"It was my time to push the cart," said Chad.

"No, it was mine," Jon replied.

"Can it!" Rand said tersely. "I'll push the cart." He looked around, clearly expecting to find Amanda missing. Instead the little girl was standing patiently beside him, her head tipped to one side as she observed the bedlam. "Amanda, would you like to push the cart?"

She looked shyly up at him. "No thank you. I'd rather help get the stuff off the shelves."

"Oh." Rand assumed by that remark that Jordon allowed her daughter to help her shop. He turned back to the boys, but they weren't there! His first thought was that they had been kidnapped. His lungs seemed to constrict, and he felt a hot, quick surge of fear rush through his body. "Amanda," he said as calmly as he could manage, "did you see which way your brothers went?"

"Uh-huh." She nodded, then pointed to Rand's right. He turned, then immediately wondered why the hell it had ever occurred to him that a kidnapper would be stupid enough to snatch the boys. For as he'd been turning, and while he watched helplessly, a sea of red as fine as Moses parting the Red Sea swept over the boys . . . in the form of Red Delicious apples . . . hitting the floor and going *bong! bong!*—in every imaginable direction.

Jordon snuggled deeper beneath the covers, refusing to allow whatever that awful noise was to rouse her completely. She'd been having the most delightful dream about a tall man with dark blond hair and the most remarkable blue eyes. She'd been running down a sandy beach toward him. The wind had been in her face, and the spray off the water had given her lips a salty taste. But just as she reached her knight and he swept her high up into his arms, the pounding became louder, waking her.

She lifted her head a fraction and listened. Even though she was still woozy from the medication, she could tell that it was definitely someone pounding on something. And it was coming from the front door. Couldn't be Rand and the kids, Jordon thought, frowning as she held her head in her hands. Didn't he have her keys? Oh, well. She sighed with annoyance. He could have lost them. She'd better check it out.

As she automatically reached for her robe on the foot of the bed, Jordon realized she still had on the shirt and slacks she'd dressed in earlier. She weaved her way unsteadily on through the house, anxious to get whoever it was on their way. The pill hadn't worn off yet, and she was still very sleepy. In her groggy state caution was the last thing she was thinking of. Without even asking who it was, she reached the door, opened it, and stood staring at the man standing there.

W. C.? Was it W. C.? It had been several years since she'd seen him, but he still looked the same.

"Hello, Mrs. Maxwell," the portly gentleman in the bowler hat nodded. "It's so good seeing you again after all these years." He tucked his umbrella under his arm and picked up his bag. "May I come in?"

"Ce-certainly," Jordon replied haltingly, and stepped aside. "Forgive me, W. C., but I'm not at my best. Have you spoken with Rand?"

"Oh, yes, madam." He smiled. "Mr. Maxwell called and explained the entire situation to me. Since I'd never been south, I decided this was the perfect time for me to do a bit of traveling." Privately he was wondering exactly what the score was. Why hadn't his boss mentioned his arrival? W. C. shrewdly regarded Jordon and decided that she definitely should be in bed. He sat his bag on the floor, then leaned his umbrella against it. "Why don't you go back and lie down, Mrs. Maxwell, and let me make you a cup of hot tea and bring it to you?"

"That sounds like a winner, W. C." She smiled sleepily. "I think I'll do just that. Though for the life of me I can't remember Rand telling me that you were coming."

"When we spoke, madam, Mr. Maxwell mentioned that you'd lost your housekeeper for an indefinite period of time. We thought I might be able to help out while Mrs. Clayton is away —that is, if you have no objections."

"Oh, no," Jordon murmured, "I have no objections." She turned toward her bedroom, her step still a bit unsteady. "Now, if you'll excuse me, W. C., I must get back to bed."

"Certainly, madam." He nodded. W. C. watched, concerned, as she left the room and then followed at a discreet distance in case she needed help. When he saw that she indeed did get back into bed, he turned and slowly began to make his way through the house. He'd been expecting chaos; what he found was a quiet disorder. Fine, he told himself. He'd have the mistress, the children, and the house in tip-top shape in no time. He would have to learn something about the area, he decided, but that shouldn't prove difficult. There was a feeling lurking within him that his boss was more than a little interested in Mrs. Maxwell. That being the case, he concluded, there would be no telling how long he would be nanny-cum-house-keeper to Mrs. Maxwell and the three little tots.

W. C. was in the kitchen, putting away the last of the breakfast dishes, when he heard a car stop in the driveway beside the house and a succession of car doors slamming. Moments later the back door flew open, and Jon and Chad, each struggling with a bag of groceries, burst into the room. They were closely followed by Rand, both his arms full, and Amanda, lugging a bag of potatoes.

"W. C.!" Rand exclaimed the moment he saw the familiar bulk of his employee and friend. "Damn, but it's good to see you." He dumped the groceries onto the table, then caught the Englishman's outstretched hand and practically dislocated the wrist from pumping it so hard. "Damn good."

"It's nice seeing you as well, sir." W. C. smiled, studying his employer's face. He'd nursed Rand through many a hangover, stood as a buffer between him and any number of women, and performed various other "rescue" acts during his time in the Maxwell household. This, however, was the first time he'd ever seen this particularly haunted look in the usually inscrutable blue eyes. "These must be the little ones, Amanda, Jon, and Chad. My name is W. C. I work for your father, and now I've come to stay with you for a while. I'll be taking Mrs. Clayton's place."

Before the words were out of his mouth, the two boys were all over him, helping him with the groceries, asking him if he played baseball, if he knew how to fish, if he liked football, and a million other questions. Rand watched their easy acceptance of W. C. and was surprised to find himself experiencing a shaft of jealousy.

The slight tug on his sleeve caused him to glance down. Amanda was looking up at him, her thumb in her mouth. Rand bent down and caught her up into his arms, rubbing his chin against the silkiness of her head. "Something wrong, princess?"

"I liked it better when you were taking care of us, Daddy," she said solemnly. "Are you going away for a long time again?"

Rand felt as if he were looking into Jordon's eyes. They were direct, without guile, and incredibly beautiful. A huge feeling of warmth swelled in his chest, constricting his throat and threatening to choke him. "Oh, no, Mandy, sweetheart, I'm not going away for a long time ever again. Is that all right with you?"

"Yes, Daddy." She smiled, then threw her tiny arms around his neck and squeezed as tightly as she could. "Now," she said, all businesslike, "I have to go and help the others."

"Of course," Rand said with a straight face as he set her on her feet and watched her hurry over and join the fray. He met W. C.'s understanding gaze over the heads of the children. It was as if both knew and understood the other's feelings . . . which they did. Rand turned and left the room, wondering how he was going to explain to Jordon about W. C. and why she hadn't been consulted.

CHAPTER SEVEN

The muted sounds of children's voices floated in and out of Jordon's mind as she worked at the breakfast-room table. Paperwork of all descriptions was strewn on the surface, and Jordan was rather appalled at the amount of work that had stacked up during her absence. It had been two weeks to the day since her accident, but she had a sinking feeling that it would be months before she would be caught up again. She was anxious to get back to the office. With W. C.'s excellent care of her and the children, her recuperation was coming along much faster than the doctors had expected. In another few days she hoped to be back at work.

In order to get even a peek at what was in store for her when her period of convalescence was over, however, she'd been forced to resort to a variety of persuasive acts, none of which had brought the slightest hint of results. Everyone, and mainly Rand, had turned a deaf ear to her pleadings . . . until she'd threatened to return to work in a far shorter time than the doctor recommended. Within mere hours a scowling Rand had personally escorted her to the kitchen and waved a large hand at the table and its burden of paper. She'd been steadily working ever since.

"Happy now?" a voice asked testily.

Jordon looked up and saw Rand standing in the doorway, each side of his mouth drawn in disapprovingly. He'd been to his hotel and showered and changed into a navy sweater and trousers in the same color. Jordon thought she'd never seen him more attractive. He walked over to where she was sitting and leaned against the sturdy table, his muscled thigh brushing her arm, making it difficult to keep her mind on her business.

"Yes," she said simply. She was tired but relaxed. Her less than enthusiastic reply surprised Rand. He peered down at her suspiciously.

"Damn it, Jordon, are you feeling worse?"

"No." She quickly shook her head, surprised by the question.

"Has something happened to upset you? Are the kids bothering you?"

"How can they?" she asked, amazed. "W. C. does a marvelous job of looking after them. Why?"

"You don't sound right," Rand muttered. "You've been going on about your damn mail and all this work. I thought you'd probably jump up and down when you finally got your way."

Suddenly a light bulb went off in her head. Of course, she thought, finally beginning to understand. Rand was disappointed. He'd done something to please her, and her reaction wasn't what he thought it would be. Why not? her conscience asked. Is it so difficult to understand his disappointment? Even sexy, towering, successful business tycoons need to feel appreciated. *Be honest. With all that's transpired between Rand and you during these past two weeks, are you really that surprised by his actions?*

"If I sound less than enthusiastic," she began, trying to mend fences, "it's because I'm still shocked. From the way you talked this morning when I mentioned needing to look over a few files, I was convinced I would be facing certain bankruptcy before I would be allowed to begin." She surprised him—and herself—by leaning forward and kissing him on the cheek. "Thank you."

"Not so fast, honey," he began huskily when she started to draw back. He stood, then pulled her to her feet. He caught her arms and eased them around his waist, then dropped his hands over the pivotal slimness of her hips and edged her closer to him. "I could get used to that."

"It was only a kiss on the cheek," Jordan murmured, embarrassed, but deep inside she wondered if that was all it had been. Being around Rand every day until late each evening when he went to his hotel had added an electricity to the atmosphere that dismayed Jordon. For if ever there was a man she hadn't the slightest chance of having a future with, it was Rand. Yet he fascinated her. And though she was aware that he continued to distrust her, she was still very attracted to him. She couldn't begin to fathom the weird reasoning behind her feelings. But they were feelings she would be forced to deal with, and soon.

"I know," he said, smiling, "and very nicely done too. Now I'm going to kiss you but not on the cheek." He lowered his head, and Jordon closed her eyes, her lips parting willingly as his mouth took possession. His tongue went straight to the sensitive points inside her mouth, caressing her own tongue, and then began tracing the outline of her lips.

His tongue moved like quicksilver, darting, tasting, arousing her to fever pitch, then, just as quickly, soothing her, lulling her into a false security before beginning again. His hands skimmed along the contours of her body, lightly touching and caressing her neck, her breasts, before molding themselves to the curve of her buttocks and pressing her closer and closer to his hips.

It was the slamming of the back door and the eruption of a disheveled Chad into the room that brought a halt to the emotion-packed moment. Jordon felt as though she had been snatched from the crumbling edge of a cliff. The child came to an abrupt halt in the middle of the kitchen, his dirt-smeared face full of surprise when he saw his mother in his father's arms.

"Do mommas and daddies that are divorced

still kiss on each other?" he asked with his usual bluntness.

"Sometimes," Rand answered as he slowly released Jordon, then moved so that he was standing beside her, one arm casually clasped to her waist. "Do you mind if I kiss her?"

"Not me." Chad shrugged. "But I betcha Cody does. I've seen Cody kiss Mommy too."

"Ah, yes." Rand nodded grimly. "Cody Grimes." His eyes turned to brilliant chips of blue ice. "I remember him from the hospital."

"Do you need something, Chad?" Jordon spoke up, hoping to stave off any further revelations by her son. Rand should remember Cody, she thought, considering that he'd acted like a child when Cody—or Hank or Tray, for that matter—had visited her.

"Just some water."

"Hurry up and get it, honey, then go back out to play. I still have loads of work to do, and I really need to get back to it."

"Afraid he'll tell more of your little secrets if you let him stay?" Rand leaned forward and whispered in her ear while Chad was gulping down a huge glass of water, then threw them a cheeky grin and scampered from the room.

"No," she replied simply. "But neither do I want him questioned. The children are friends with all the men I date. I think that's best for all concerned." She turned and faced him. "That way, when I remarry, the transition won't be so traumatic for the kids."

His arm at her waist tightened so fiercely and

so quickly, Jordon gasped with pain. "What the hell do you mean 'remarry'?" he thundered. Emotionally Rand was shocked to the core. She talked about marrying in the same vein as going to the grocery store for a dozen eggs, he thought in amazement. Worse still, that she spoke the word at all made him furious. Besides, he told himself piously, he wasn't sure he wanted the children subjected to a stepfather.

"Exactly what it sounds like," she returned in an equally loud voice. "Will you please let go of me?" she said, squirming. "You're about to crack one of my ribs."

Rand released her, but he didn't bother apologizing. Nor was he likely to later, he thought sourly. She had no business springing something like marriage on him. "Just how long has that crazy idea been floating around in that vacant head of yours?" he snapped.

Jordon stepped back, put off by the rudeness of his expression and the tone of his voice. "Let's get something straight here and now, Rand," she said quietly. She would have preferred to continue yelling just as loud as he'd done and calling him a few choice names to boot, but the children were right outside, and she didn't want them upset. "This is my house, and while you are in it you will not scream at me and tell me that my head is vacant. Understand?"

"How long, Jordon?" he persisted, as if he hadn't heard a single word she'd just spoken.

His hands had turned to round, wicked-look-ing fists, resting uneasily on his hips.

Oooh! The damn man was hopeless. "I don't know for how long," she said with a sigh. "As they get older I realize the children need a father. It's quite simple, really." She turned around and sat back down at the table, praying that he'd take the hint and leave.

"There's nothing simple about it at all. And in case you've forgotten—though for the life of me I can't see how, what with all the trouble you've gone to to remind me—the children have a father." He paused, then growled. "Which one is it?"

She looked up at him, puzzled. "I beg your pardon?"

"Which of the three men that visited you in the hospital are you thinking of marrying?" he demanded. He braced his hands against the table and leaned menacingly toward her, but for some reason Jordon didn't feel in the least threatened. She was, however, very much amused. Determined and ornery, he might be, she mused, but he wasn't a cruel man.

"Oh," she murmured in feigned vagueness. "Actually I haven't decided yet, Rand. What about you? You met each of them. Do you hap-pen to have a particular preference? The kids like all three."

"You're a few years behind the times, lady. These days it's against the law to have more than one husband," he snapped, so hard that Jordon was surprised his teeth didn't fall out.

119

"Frankly I don't think much of your idea. How can you possibly take care of our children while you're shopping and comparing men?"

"*Our* children, Rand?" she asked mockingly. "Surely there must be something wrong with my hearing."

"I doubt it."

"But you said *our* children." She stared levelly at him, for the moment forgetting the amusing notion of teasing him. She was still involved with the fight to have their children acknowledged by him, and twice within the last few seconds he'd done exactly that. She wanted to hear it again—coming directly from him and in answer to a direct question from her!

Rand looked past her shoulder toward the window that looked out over the backyard where the triplets were playing. There was an expression of chagrin on his face that would have been comical under any other circumstances, Jordon decided. She could see first-hand that eating crow wasn't one of Rand's favorite things, especially a crow that had had six and a half years in which to grow as tough as leather. But this wasn't the time for sympathy, she quickly admonished herself. "After all this time are you honestly saying the children are yours, Rand?"

"Why, of course," he replied, as if she were being silly for asking. "I also think it's time I started taking advantage of my visitation rights given me in our divorce."

"One weekend a month, six weeks in the summer, and alternate Christmases," Jordon supplied without hesitation. "You also are required to make certain that your visitation is convenient for me, as well as the children," she reminded him.

Suddenly the thought of the triplets being away from her for six weeks left Jordon with a sick feeling in the pit of her stomach. She was delighted that Rand finally seemed to admit to being their father. But did he have to go completely crazy? Or was he doing it just to annoy her? "Would you like to start this weekend?"

"Got a hot date with Cody?" Rand retaliated savagely.

"No, I do not, and even if I did, I fail to see why you should get so angry about it. Haven't you had your share of women since we were divorced?" she asked curiously, amazed to find that the question left her feeling rather like a truck had hit her. It occurred to Jordon that thinking of Rand making love to another woman, and having that thought bring pain to her, was most peculiar. Why should she care what he did with his free time?

"What has the number of women I've dated since we divorced got to do with this conversation?" he asked haughtily.

"About the same thing as you going into a flap because I mentioned marrying again," she retaliated.

"I think we should discuss it," he said grudgingly, refusing to meet the open frankness of her brown eyes.

"Certainly. But another time, okay? Right now I need to finish this work."

Rand started to protest, but Jordon had already turned away. He felt like someone who had been dismissed. It didn't sit well with him, he thought. He'd much rather discuss her notion of remarrying. It was a loose end, he kept repeating to himself as he walked outside where the children were playing with W. C., and he didn't want any loose threads tangling up his life.

Though the subject of her remarrying wasn't actually broached in the following days, it became an unspoken bone of contention between Rand and Jordon, which Jordon began to resent.

"Just who the hell does he think he is?" she exploded on more than one occasion to Ellie over a cup of coffee. It was Jordon's second day back at work, and she was tired but enjoying herself. She'd worked only till two-thirty and planned on keeping that schedule for the remainder of the first week. After that she felt a normal week wouldn't be too much.

"Sounds to me like the words of a jealous man," Ellie offered with a cheeky grin.

"That's ridiculous," Jordon sputtered. Really! There were times when she wondered about Ellie. "Need I repeat any of the story you've heard a thousand times already?"

"Please"—Ellie held up her hands in self-defense—"I know the story from start to finish. It was a lousy thing for the man to do, but has it ever occurred to you that there were a lot of things wrong with that marriage?"

"It had, and there were." Jordon sighed. "In the first place I was so spoiled, it wasn't funny. And when Rand made demands on me that smacked of the slightest responsibility, I panicked. No wonder he thought that I was having an affair with Jason. I practically lived at Jason's apartment. Always either angry or crying or both. I'm surprised Jason didn't move and forget to tell me his new address."

"Don't be so anxious to take all the blame, honey, just because Rand's finally decided to accept the children. From where I sit, the marriage was jinxed before it got off the ground."

"My, you sound experienced." Jordon chuckled.

"Ah, yes, my colorful past, you know." Ellie grinned. "Seriously, though, I know Rand has made you angry as sin, but try looking at him as a man and not as *just* the father of your children for a change."

"I've already done that," Jordon murmured resignedly.

"And?"

"It was devastating."

"Good, good," Ellie almost squealed with excitement. "See? If you let yourself, you just might fall in love with him. Why not add him to your stable of 'eligibles' and see what happens?"

"Christ! You make it sound like I'm some sort of sex maniac. And besides that, Rand might not take too kindly to being lumped with the other men I know. Frankly I'm more inclined to think that he would want to be the only man in a woman's life. We were married less than a year, but even in that short period of time I remember a few things about him. Darn." She frowned as she glanced down at her watch. "What happened to the time? I've got to scoot, Ellie. I'll give you a ring tomorrow."

During the morning and into the afternoon, Ellie's advice kept winging its way through Jordon's thoughts, and each time it did, she tried her best to put it out of her mind. She and Rand had hurt each other so much, it was highly improbable that either of them could ever completely forget the past enough to want another chance at a future together.

When Cody Grimes called just before she was ready to leave the office and asked her to have coffee with him, Jordon gladly accepted. He'd dropped by the house a couple of times after she got home from the hospital, but each visit was marred by Rand, who acted as if Cody were a leper.

"How's it going?" Cody asked as Jordon slipped into the chair opposite him. The restaurant, caught between lunch and dinner, was virtually empty except for two tables of tourists.

"Great." She grinned. "I think. Frankly I'm bushed."

Cody sat back down and smiled at her. "It's good to see you without your former husband's scowling face leering menacingly at me. How do you put up with that joker?"

"After a while he wears on you," she said lightly. "I think I'll have a piece of cheesecake with my coffee," she said to the hovering waiter. "How is the world of bulging biceps and lean, lithe bodies?" Cody owned two successful fitness centers in the city.

"We're making it." He nodded. "How long before you'll be back to normal with your schedule?"

"Next week, I think. Each day the work is getting a little easier, as my doctor has assured me it will continue to do. If I find it too much to stay all day, then I'll simply rearrange my schedule so that it fits my needs."

The waiter appeared with coffee and cheesecake for them both. After he'd gone, Jordon tasted the dessert, then closed her eyes appreciatively. "This is delicious."

"I'm glad to see that your appetite hasn't suffered," Cody quipped. "The amount of food you eat and your ability to remain slim amaze me."

"You're not glad," she shot right back, "you're jealous."

"So I am," he said with a sigh. "I hate to bring up unpleasant subjects, but has there been a trial date set for the hoodlums that robbed the grocery store and shot you and that manager?"

"According to Rand, the trial is scheduled sometime within the next three months. The court docket is crammed. In the meantime the four stooges get to enjoy lodgings courtesy of the parish. Honestly, Cody, if only you could have heard and seen those four. They were so stupid, it would have been funny if it hadn't been so terrifying."

Cody nodded. They talked about first one thing and then another. It was an easy, relaxed conversation, and Jordon found herself enjoying it.

"Have dinner with me this evening?" Cody asked suddenly.

"Sounds nice but not tonight. How about a rain check?"

"Afraid of making Rand Maxwell angry? By the way, do you have any idea how much that man is worth?"

"No, I'm not afraid of making Rand angry." Jordon smiled. "And from the sound of your voice he must be worth quite a bundle."

"I often wondered how you were able to own your own home and afford a full-time housekeeper. Now I know."

White-hot anger surged throughout every fiber of Jordon's being at the crude insinuation. She would never have dreamed Cody capable of such a remark. "You owe me an apology, mister," she said crisply. "I make my own way. Rand pays child support, and that's all."

"Come on, Jordon," he said, disbelieving. "This is old Cody, honey; you don't have to pretend with me. So what if you're getting a hefty alimony check from Maxwell. I think it's great. And if you're smart, you'll get your lawyer to go for the cost of living increase every two years."

Unable to adequately express herself because of her fury, Jordon quietly pushed back her chair and stood. "Good-bye, Cody," she said in a cool, firm voice. "And please don't bother calling me again."

"Hey, Jordon!" He rose to his feet hastily. "I was kidding, okay?"

"No, you weren't," Jordon countered. "See you around, Cody." She turned and walked out of the restaurant, wishing that she had the strength to break every bone in Cody Grimes's body.

The moment she entered her back door, Jordon wondered fleetingly if some mysterious malady had befallen her three wild Indians. The house was as quiet as a tomb. Too quiet, she decided. She dropped her briefcase and purse on the table, then walked into the kitchen and poured herself a cup of coffee. Just as she was adding sugar and cream, she heard the muffled sound of footsteps in the hallway.

"Who's there?" she called out. When there was no answer, she edged a step or two closer to the table that was between her and the back door. "Rand? Sid?"

The sight of Rand, dressed only in pants and shoes, materializing in the doorway, caused Jordon to slump, relieved, against the table. "Do you have to creep around like a damn spook?" she asked as soon as her heartbeat returned to normal.

Rand held his chin higher, letting her see the nails he was holding between his lips. By then Jordon was staring at the hammer, expandable ruler, and various other tools he was carrying in his hands. A grunt was all he was able to manage.

"Sorry." She shrugged as she pulled out a chair and sat down. "What were you repairing?"

After depositing the tools on a shelf in the small closet in the laundry room, Rand joined her. "The door to Mandy's closet was sticking, and Jon somehow managed to jam the bottom drawer of his chest. I'm sure Chad will come up with something by tomorrow, since they seem to do everything pretty much in threes. The kids are with W. C." He leaned back in his chair, and Jordon could barely take her eyes off him.

Even though it was early fall and the nights had begun to cool considerably, the days were still warm and lazy for the most part. Rand, being a hot-natured person, had removed his shirt, and there was nothing at all to keep her from seeing and remembering the breadth of his shoulders, the dark blond pelt of hair cov-

128

ering his chest, and how it felt to lay her cheek against that rough, furry pillow.

"Th-that was nice of you," she began, hardly aware of her lips and tongue moving, not to mention that she hadn't the slighest idea what she was saying. She felt hypnotized. That's it, she thought, bemused. She was hypnotized. Rand had done something she was unaware of, and it had caused her to slip into a trance.

His chest was so brown. But, no; she quickly compared his face with the rest of him, and she could see that he wasn't any darker than he used to be. She'd always envied him his ability to tan. Jon and Chad had his coloring.

"Jordon?" It was one thing to be stared at, Rand was thinking, but another to watch her go off into a trance. Was she ill? he thought worriedly. "Jordon? Are you all right?" He let the chair come down on all four legs, then leaned forward and snapped his fingers in front of her eyes. "Jordon?" he said more urgently.

She jumped. "What? Oh." She looked around, embarrassed. "I'm sorry, I was thinking about something," she murmured. She took a sip of the coffee and grimaced. She'd forgotten to stir it.

Rand made no further comment. He didn't have to. Whether or not she was aware of it, there had been an open invitation in her eyes for him to take her in his arms. An invitation he would have liked very much to accept if he didn't know that the kids and W. C. were due back any minute. "Are you busy this evening?" he asked quietly.

"No." Jordon shook her head. "Why?"

"Would you have dinner with me?"

"Why?" she asked, and could have cut out her tongue the moment the words were out of her mouth.

"You're an attractive woman. I enjoy being with you. Is that enough?" Rand smiled. "Or would you like for me to go on?"

"I think I get the message." She looked away, a slight flush sweeping over her features.

"By the way, your friend Cody Grimes called right before you got home. He asked for you to call him as soon as you got in." He'd never seen her looking more beautiful, Rand was thinking. Hot, aching desire began snaking its way over him. Even if it might totally wipe him out, he wanted Jordon.

"Er . . . thanks. What time do you want to go out?" Jordon looked at him and wished with all her heart that she hadn't. His eyes were like blue pools of fire, their smoldering brilliance pulling at something inside her.

"Let's make a long evening of it. Why don't we plan on leaving around seven? That'll give us plenty of time for a nice leisurely dinner, maybe a little dancing. Who knows?" He knew he was going to make love to her before the night was over.

"Sounds like fun." She was a fool. An utter and complete fool.

"Are you going to call Grimes?"

"No."

"Why not?" Rand asked curiously. He'd seen the flash of temper in her eyes and wondered what was wrong.

"Nothing of importance," she said, hedging. She stood and then walked over and placed her cup and saucer in the dishwasher. "We had a disagreement this afternoon."

"Was it about me?" Rand spoke from just behind her, and Jordon started at the sudden sound of his voice, so close to her.

She stared out the window, waiting for the touch of his hands. When it came, she could feel her body relaxing from one plane, yet becoming excited—becoming poised for another, more devastating flight. "Yes. But I took care of it."

"What was it? What did he say?" The steely tone let her know that he wasn't likely to stop till he was satisfied. His broad palms skimmed down over her hips, the material of her skirt feeling crisp against his skin. She was so damned tiny, he thought idly, so tiny. So small yet so volatile. Could she possibly hold his happiness in her hands?

"He wouldn't believe that I wasn't getting alimony from you. He'd thought so all along. When I denied it, he made the whole thing sound ugly, as if I were some kind of leech with my eye on your bankroll. He surprised me . . . I guess you could say he even hurt me. Losing a friend makes me sad."

Rand slowly turned her around to him, his

131

hands going up and framing her face. "I think the only thing that matters is that I know you aren't interested in my money. You've never been, and I'll tell that to Cody Grimes if it will make you happy," he said huskily. "In the meantime let's begin thinking of ways to spend some of my fortune on the evening ahead. After I kiss you again, that is." His lips met hers in a message that was as true, as obvious, as the hardness of his thighs pressed intimately against hers. Jordon felt the brilliant warmth of desire merging with her need for this man. The depth of her passion shocked her to her very soul.

CHAPTER EIGHT

There were feelings of ambivalence stirring in Jordon's thoughts during her dinner with Rand. She carried on what she hoped was a sensible conversation on her part. It was weird, she told herself as she sat across the table from him, fascinated with the way the candlelight cast shadows upon his rough-hewn features.

For years she'd spent a few moments of each day thinking of her hatred for Rand. Mulling over it, nurturing it. In her mind she'd concocted all sorts of cruel and inhuman punishments for him. Six months ago, even three months ago, if someone had told her that she would be having dinner with him and seriously considering going to bed with him, she would have been highly insulted. Now, finding herself doing just that, she could only shake her head and wonder at human nature.

"No dessert till you've eaten at least three more bites of your veal," Rand said, breaking into her thoughts.

Jordon looked away quickly, feeling rather foolish to have been caught staring for the second time. Finally she turned back to Rand, more confident than a moment ago, and smiled. "I'm a few years older than the triplets. You don't have to bribe me in order to get me to eat."

It was his turn to look uncomfortable. "Sorry. I haven't the slightest idea what it is about you that makes me want to protect you, but I do."

"It's a lovely thought, Rand," Jordon said. "And without your help these past few weeks I have no idea what I would have done. But I think, somewhere in the back of your mind, that you're still confusing me with the Jordon you knew when my father died."

"That sounds like a polite way of telling me you don't need my help any longer. Is that what you're saying?" He leaned back in his chair and regarded her lazily. Maybe she had a point, Rand thought as he studied her. Lately he had been having difficulty separating the two Jordons in his mind. The new Jordon—or perhaps she was the real Jordon, the one he'd never gotten to know—was a very heady lady. He could barely keep his hands off her. Images of her naked in his arms constantly floated in and out of his mind. Even now, with a room full of people all around them, Rand knew he wanted nothing more than to scoop her up into his arms and take her to his hotel. The tiny, narrow straps and the deep neckline of the peach silk dress she was wearing, accentuating the gentle swell of her breasts, caught and held his possessive gaze.

"Are you through eating?" he asked suddenly.

Jordon looked surprised. "What's wrong? Don't you feel well?"

"No. I'm in pain. I feel terrible." He signaled the waiter for their check, and within minutes a dazed Jordon stood beside Rand as they waited for his car.

"Can I do anything for you?" she asked, concerned. "Is the pain really bad?"

A low chuckle filled her ears, and a long arm went snugly around her waist and pulled her tightly against the tall, hard length of him. "The pain is unbelievable, and I sincerely hope you will help me, honey. But not here."

"I don't think—" Jordan began, only to become silent as his insinuation fully struck her and his low, husky laughter echoed in her ears. "That's awful," she said after a moment, but for all her protestations there was no denying the sparkle in her dark eyes, nor the way she didn't bother moving away from Rand.

Why should she? she thought fleetingly.

"Will you stop by my hotel with me?" he asked, his lips pressed against her hair.

"Yes."

One simple word. Yet Rand couldn't remember ever hearing anything that sounded sweeter. He slipped a hand beneath Jordon's chin and made her look at him. "I don't plan on giving you a quick tour and then taking you home. You do know that, don't you?" He wanted no surprises. More than that, he didn't want *her* to be surprised. They had become friends; now he wanted them to become lovers.

"I know," Jordon said softly. "And though it's a very lovely, exclusive hotel," she said without blinking an eye, "for the life of me I can't imagine why I'd care to be shown around when there are other . . . more interesting, things to do."

Rand sucked in a huge gulp of air, positive that his head was going to explode. Six weeks ago he would have killed any man alive for even hinting that Rand would be taking his ex-wife to dinner, not to mention becoming her lover. When his car slammed to a stop in front of them, he didn't even glare at the young man. Instead he tipped the youth generously, saw Jordon into the passenger seat, got behind the wheel, and took off like a hot-rodder.

Twenty-five minutes later, as she stepped inside Rand's elegant suite, Jordon was unable to suppress a grin.

"What's so funny?" he asked. He removed his jacket, then took it and Jordon's light wrap and threw them over a chair.

"Me," she said, chuckling. "I've been blithely calling this place your 'room.' "

"Do you like it?"

"Who wouldn't? But only for a brief change. Believe it or not, I'm kind of partial to crab-grass, stubborn plumbing, and a messy house."

Rand caught her in his arms and kissed her.

"Are you becoming sort of fond of me, Jordon Maxwell?"

"Maybe," she murmured huskily, her eyes a tawny brown but still honest and direct. "I haven't decided yet."

Rand stepped back, still a little amazed by her power to arouse him. Her response to his question annoyed him. That she desired him was quite evident. Neither of them had been very good at hiding their emotions, he thought rationalizing. However, he wanted more from her—although he couldn't decide exactly what it was. He walked over to a narrow shelf tucked beneath the wraparound windows and pressed a button. Sliding doors whirred open, revealing a well-stocked bar. "Are you still a Philistine when it comes to good wines?"

"Completely." Jordon walked over and sat down on the plush sofa, her gaze open and relaxed. "Running after three active children doesn't leave much time for pursuing such frivolous things as learning about wines. Would you like to know about baby formulas? I'm an expert in that field."

He laughed, placing the drinks on the table in front of the sofa and dropping beside her. "I imagine they've managed to monopolize quite a bit of your life, haven't they?"

"Yes," she answered unequivocally. "But now that they've become so close with their father, and he has such a gem in W. C."—she smiled devilishly—"I'll be able to go and do some of the things I've always had to 'put off till later.' That phrase has become my own personal slogan."

"Why don't we do those things together?" Rand wasn't smiling when he asked the question. He could just imagine her on some cruise, strolling on deck with a man or lolling on a beach in a bikini while some damn jerk smeared suntan lotion on her. He took her glass from her hand and set it back on the table, then pulled her to him and settled her in his arms so that her head was resting against his chest and her legs were stretched out along the sofa. "Does that idea appeal to you?"

"Don't try to blend our futures together at this stage, Rand," Jordon said quietly. "We've made tremendous inroads toward establishing something very nice between us. I know it sounds trite, but let's do take it one day at a time."

"Afraid, Jordon?" he murmured harshly.

"Yes" was her blunt reply. "Aren't you?"

For a moment Rand appeared displeased, then he shrugged. "I suppose I am." He reached for his glass and downed the rest of his drink. "How did we suddenly get so serious? I brought you here to make love to you." He looked down into her eyes and found the same longing he was feeling.

"Yes . . . I know."

"And that doesn't frighten you?"

"Oh, no. Quite the contrary, in fact." She pushed herself up on one elbow, then reached up and loosened his tie and removed it. Next she began unbuttoning his shirt, not stopping till his hair-covered chest was bare and the shirt pushed off his shoulders. "In case you've suddenly been stricken with a case of conscience, please put it aside. I want this just as much as you do, and I have no intention of feeling guilty afterward."

"Is this new boldness of yours derived from practice," Rand asked in a curiously flat voice, "or are you trying to get back at Cody Grimes by going to bed with me?"

"Neither, Rand," Jordon said distinctly. "It's really quite simple. I remember your being one heck of a lover. We might have fought most of our time together, but those rare moments when we were loving have their place in my memory as well. It's also been a very long time since I've been to bed with a man."

For a second Rand simply stared. He couldn't quite figure out if he'd been complimented or was about to be used. At the moment, however, he really didn't care. One hand had already found its way beneath the abbreviated neckline and was teasing the hot, stiff tips of her breasts. Backing off at this stage was impossible.

Jordon's hands against his chest clenched and unclenched in rapid succession as his tongue replaced his marauding fingers. He was skillfully coercing a smoldering coal into a flame, and by its every gesture and move, Jordon's body was pleading with him to fan that flame into a raging inferno.

Rand sensed her desire for him mounting as rapidly as his was leaping out of control for her. He felt it in her soft, pliant body, in the way her hands caught his head and drew his mouth down to hers—to her eagerly seeking tongue. He heard it in the tiny moaning sounds she was making, sounds he was mouthing and absorbing into his own being. He rose to his feet, bearing Jordon's weight with the slightest effort, and strode determinedly to the bedroom.

As he sat her on her feet beside the king-size bed and his large hands clasped her waist, then eased upward to the sides of her breasts, the restriction of clothing became unbearable to Rand. Hastily, without regard for buttons or fabric, Jordon's dress soon became a silken, peach-colored heap beside the bed, along with her panty hose. Rand's own clothes quickly followed. His eyes swept hungrily over the pointed, thrusting nipples, which reminded him of two small, dark rubies. He sat on the edge of the bed and pulled Jordon between his legs. With an almost worshipful gleam in his eyes his hands lifted the weight of her breasts, his mouth eagerly seeking out the jeweled tips.

The sucking, pulling sensation caused by his lips and tongue created a spiraling explosion of desire inside her body. Even her fingers, buried in the thickness of his hair, tingled as if she'd received some sort of electrical shock. Her toes curled tightly against the carpet, and her knees became rubbery.

A maelstrom of ecstasy was surrounding her, and Jordon was positive that she was going to fall, but somehow she didn't. When she felt the hot tip of Rand's tongue leaving a random trail of warm, moist kisses across her stomach, the muscles of her abdomen tightened spasmodically, and there was a curious quivering of her hips.

"Ple-please," she murmured brokenly. Once the plea was uttered, she wasn't sure exactly what she was asking.

"Please . . . what?" Rand said roughly, his breathing coming in short, husky breaths as he invaded the mystery of her femininity, protected by the satiny smoothness of her inner thighs. "Jordon, talk to me. Tell me what you want."

God! He wanted her so badly, his entire body was beginning to jerk. Tiny rivulets of perspiration were working their way down the middle of his back. But, he told himself, he would not take her till he was convinced that there would be no turning back on her part. Their sexual attraction for each other had become his unwitting ace in the hole where Jordon was concerned.

Inwardly Rand refused to consider the less than honorable connotations associated with his actions. The skin beneath his hands, the gentle curves that outlined her body slipping in and out of his touch, was like fire in his blood. When his lips singled out that most intimate part of her and he heard her soft moan of pleasure, his pulse began to hammer.

In his life he'd learned to take the breaks where he found them. And while his relationship with Jordon was an entirely different matter, in a sense the same principles applied. It was pure and simple, he rationalized. Over the past few weeks he'd become fascinated with the beautiful, poised woman who'd once been his wife. He wanted a relationship with her . . . some hold on her that would prevent her from neatly dealing him out of her future. Yet he was sensitive enough to Jordon's feelings to know that time was needed to heal the emotional scars he'd inflicted upon her. Rand thought of the moment when she'd said she was considering remarrying. He still wasn't sure he had recovered from that shock. He wanted Jordon . . . and he'd do whatever was necessary to get her and to hold her.

Rand collapsed against the bed, bringing Jordon with him, their arms and legs writhing in a sensuous tangle. Her silken skin sought the roughness of his; the coarse, curly growth on his chest was like a supercharged electrode against the highly sensitive tips of Jordon's breasts.

"Are you sure this is what you want, Jordon?" Rand found enough presence of mind to ask. His lips were touching her face with quick, light kisses that were driving Jordon out of her mind with anticipation.

"Mmmm," she murmured in throaty consent, at the moment involved with catching his head and bringing his mouth down to hers. She kissed him then, long and deep and hard, feeling a flicker of pain from the pressure of her inner lip scraping against the sharp edge of his teeth. He'd awakened a slumbering river of desire inside her, and she was unable to control her actions. Indeed she hadn't the slightest desire to do so.

Without the slightest effort Rand turned her on her back, then positioned himself between her thighs, his arms going around her and cradling her. When Jordon opened her eyes and looked into his, only an inch or so above hers, she was startled. In the depths of passion Rand's eyes had turned a deep, blue-gray. There was a glowing intensity, combined with some nameless, primitive aura reaching out to her in his gaze.

Jordon didn't look away . . . she couldn't. When the hardness of his manhood entered and filled her, she whimpered, her eyes narrowing with the inexplicable rush of wonder spilling over her. The next few minutes became a space of incredible beauty, potent surges, and powerful explosions as each gave and took, as each made love to the other.

It had been a week now since that night Jordon and Rand had made love. A week during which she'd had dinner with him two other times and had seen him almost daily. She'd also gone out with Tray Gentry during the

143

week. Tray was nice, and she honestly thought she would enjoy being with him, but her thoughts had stayed on Rand. Afterward Jordon told herself it was silly to waste her time with other men until she had her feelings worked out concerning Rand. It would also prove less nerve-racking. Rand was quite open with his disapproval and even had the gall to wait at her house till Tray brought her home.

She sighed, her fingers going to her temples that were beginning to throb, she was sure, from trying to do so much paperwork in one evening. One part of her was secretly thrilled by this attention from a man who'd once treated her so cruelly. The other part of her was still smarting from that unfair treatment and was annoyed that he thought he could wipe away all the hurt by a few weeks of devoted attention.

Frankly, she decided, she needed space. Just as she'd wanted to go to bed with Rand, she needed a few days away from him. It looked to her, though, as if he had no intention of ever returning to Denver, which bothered her. She looked down at the report she was holding in her hand but was unable to concentrate on the figures before her. Rand had a tendency to embrace each thing that interested him, much the same way he did with the huge corporation he'd built . . . with a single-mindedness that was awesome. Jordon knew that if she wasn't strong where he was concerned, he would be controlling her life. And to what end? she asked herself.

The small bell attached to the outer door of the office sounded, and Jordon looked beyond the glass-and-wood partition separating her desk from the rest of the office, toward the front. She smiled and waved at Ellie, who was walking toward her. "Have I missed a day?" Jordon quipped. "You aren't suppose to be back till tomorrow."

Ellie, dazzling in a pale blue designer suit, dropped into the only other chair in the cubicle and briefly closed her eyes. "I'm just getting in," she said after a moment. "We finished a day ahead of schedule. I have yet to figure out what's so delightful about Florida. It's hot and sandy. I always leave there feeling wrung out. What's been happening while I've been away?"

"Nothing out of the ordinary, thank goodness," Jordon said, tipping her head slightly. "Rand's still in town, as is W. C. The kids and Sid are fine, and I'm almost killing myself trying to catch up. We kept an eye on your house and watered your plants while you were gone."

"Thanks. Business good?"

"Very steady and growing. The minute you get tired of modeling, the adjoining space"—she nodded toward the corner across from her—"is yours."

"That might be sooner than you think." Ellie sighed. "I'm tired of having my life dictated by curfews, diets, and a camera. Does that sound selfish?"

"Not at all." Jordon shook her head. "You keep a grueling pace. Although, to be truthful, it's just as hectic here but in a different way. However, we do make our own decisions, and that helps."

"Sounds better all the time. Still going out with Rand?"

"Occasionally."

"What do the kids think of their mama and papa dating?"

"They giggle and whisper till I think I'm going to choke them. It would be helpful if there was some precedent from which to draw. It's a little disconcerting hearing your children discuss your dates with their father."

Ellie laughed. "I suppose it is, but it's also rather touching. Regardless of your prior problems, you and Rand are nice people, and so are your children. Now fill me in."

"About what?"

"About what's really going on between you and Rand," Ellie said without the slightest hesitation. "Is there a possibility of you remarrying? Is he opening an office in New Orleans? Are you and the triplets moving to Denver?"

"Gee." Jordon sat back in her chair, unruffled. "Is that all?"

"It's a start." Ellie frowned. "Pumping you for information is like getting water out of a stone."

"There could be a very good reason for my reticence. Could be that it's none of your business." Jordon replied in an amused voice. Re-

146

gardless of her closeness to her friend, she didn't feel inclined to talk about Rand. There were still too many unanswered questions in her own mind for her to be discussing him with Ellie.

Ellie threw her a brittle smile that spoke volumes. "You're like a damn clam. How about going to the wrestling match with me this evening?"

Jordon stared at the blonde, a look of total puzzlement on her face. "How is it possible for a woman as lovely and poised as you are to enjoy such a ridiculous spectacle as wrestling?" she asked disdainfully.

"It's different." Ellie grinned. "It also lets me unwind after a day of very tedious, demanding work. Are you going? Montana Hank sure did take a shine to you the night you went with me."

"No." Jordon shook her head. "Once was enough, and I have no desire to get to know your friend Montana any better. Besides, I'm working late."

"Meet me afterward for a late supper." She grinned. "You can fill me in on your romance with Rand, and I'll give you a play-by-play of the match."

Jordon laughed, unable to remain stern with her friend. "I'll meet you at Dario's at ten. Okay?"

Shortly after Ellie left, the two girls who worked full-time for Jordon finished for the day. She settled down to get some serious work done, for once thankful for a silent telephone. Approximately an hour had gone by with Jordon updating accounts and customer's files when there was a sudden knock on the front door.

Jordon gave a start, the unexpectedness of the noise momentarily frightening her. Ever since the hostage incident at the grocery store, she'd found herself as jumpy as a cat. She looked toward the front door, barely able to make out the shape of a tall, broad-shouldered man. And even though she couldn't see his face, Jordon knew instinctively that it was Rand.

She got up from her desk, a sigh of resignation escaping her lips. Rand hadn't been at all pleased when he'd called earlier and learned that she was going to be working late.

"Why?" he'd asked curtly. "Don't you think you should be home in the evenings with the kids?"

Jordon had almost laughed outright at the petulant timbre in his voice. Stay home in the evenings with the children, indeed! Where had he been for the last six and a half years? "Were you thinking of the children several nights ago, Rand, dear, when we spent a greater part of the evening at your apartment making love?" she asked sweetly.

"That's different," he said raspily. "I'm their father. You were with me."

"In other words, it's all right for me to be

148

away from them if I'm with you but not with anyone else. Right?"

"You're overreacting," Rand said stiffly. "However, if your career is more important to you than the welfare of the triplets, then I'll spend the evening with them."

"Good!" Jordon exclaimed. "It's about time you contributed something other than money to their development." She plunked down the receiver. It took several minutes for her to calm down enough to return to her normal duties.

So what did he want now? Jordon wondered irritably as she walked toward the front door and opened it. "Hello, Rand. I really can't say it's a pleasure seeing you here, but come in, anyway."

Rand watched her through narrowed blue eyes as he stepped inside, then closed the door with his foot. Before she could turn away, he caught her in his arms and kissed her deep and hard, then released her. "You should have something over these windows," he remarked as he followed a shaken Jordon back to her desk, his eyes sweeping warmly over her body, a body he knew as intimately as his own. The sight of her caused his blood to quicken. He was aware of a hot, reckless surge of passion growing within him; she excited him, yet she made him wary. He wasn't accustomed to being so skillfully handled by a woman . . . even one who wasn't aware of her power over him. He wondered if he'd ever get over this need for her. Would this gut-wrenching empti-ness that ate at him when she wasn't with him never leave him?

"My budget doesn't include an appropriate window covering at this point," Jordon in-formed him, hating the husky unsteadiness of her voice. Damn him! She was so tense, she could feel her fingernails biting into her palms. The scent and feel of him filled the space around her, bringing an ache deep in the pit of her stomach, an ache of desire that his kiss had merely whetted. But it wasn't only desire that brought that sense of excitement to her when she saw Rand, or the breathlessness that as-sailed her when she would stop and watch him walking toward her, or the heart-stopping completeness that filled her when he took her in his arms. She was experiencing emotions where Rand was concerned that she hadn't counted on. Emotions she'd never felt for an-other man, including the old Rand.

A peculiar rush slid over her like a douse of cold water. Was it possible that she was falling in love with Rand? Now, wouldn't that be a hoot and a half? she thought, berating herself.

"Then find an 'appropriate covering,'" he said, mimicking her, and added, "I'll pay for it." He sat on the edge of the desk, then stretched his long legs out before him and re-garded Jordon with a frown. "There're still people out there who consider you a subject of curiosity because of the incident at the grocery store. You're asking for trouble by making yourself such an available target."

"I hadn't thought about it from that standpoint," she acknowledged sheepishly, finding it difficult to face the open desire she saw in his gaze. "I'll tend to it tomorrow." Lord! He was seducing her with his very eyes, and Jordon could feel her body responding of its own will.

She picked up the first piece of paper her hand encountered and pretended an inordinate interest in it, though to be perfectly honest, she couldn't make out a single word. But at least it gave her something to do with her hands and her eyes. "Was there something specific you wanted to see me about?" she asked.

"Yes," Rand replied, then surprised her by breaking out in a husky laugh.

"What's so funny?" she demanded tersely.

Rand gently removed the paper from her hand and placed it on the desk. "You were reading it upside down."

"Oh."

"Do I bother you, Jordon?"

"Yes."

"How?"

"My stomach gets queasy, a peculiar trembling attacks my body, and my tongue becomes three inches thick."

"Sounds like a serious illness," Rand quipped dryly, though there was a definite twinkle in his eyes. He leaned sideways and caught her by her upper arms, urging her to her feet. His hold didn't leave her until she was standing between his strong, muscled thighs, his hands locked behind her waist. "I think a closer relationship with me would go a long way toward helping you get over this mysterious malady. What do you think?"

Jordon dropped her gaze to where her fingers were idly tracing patterns on the conservative striped tie he was wearing with one of the numerous dark suits he favored during office hours. His question was an ambiguous one, one she hadn't the slightest idea how to answer. "I think probably the most reliable treatment would be the same one I had when I was nine."

"Which was?"

She looked up at him and grinned. "I took shots and got rid of my tomcat."

"Well, I hate to disappoint you, sweetheart, but this tomcat has no intention of letting you 'get rid' of him." He leaned farther back, the move causing her to lose her balance and slump against him. Jordon could feel the hardness of his thighs against hers and blushed. She tried to push herself upright, but Rand would have none of that.

"I have several things to finish before I leave," she told him, trying to sound firm but failing miserably. His chest beneath her palms was vibrating with the rapid beat of his heart, and Jordon knew he was fast approaching a state of arousal that wouldn't be denied.

"Have dinner with me when you get through."

"That sounds like—oops," she burst out as she remembered her date with Ellie. "I can't. I promised Ellie I'd meet her at Dario's at ten o'clock." She glanced at the slim gold watch on her wrist. "It's nine now."

Rand was shocked to find himself jealous of a woman, but he was. He eased Jordon back, then moved away from her, his expression thunderous. "I'll be waiting for you at your place." Before Jordon could say a word, he turned and left.

CHAPTER NINE

Jordon tried to shake the guilty feeling that had settled over her. Dinner with Ellie had gone longer than either of them had expected. Ellie was in a down mood, and Jordon hadn't minded listening to her friend talk out some of her frustration. It was something they did for each other from time to time.

Once in the car heading home, though, Jordon could well imagine Rand's reaction to her being later than she'd told him she'd be.

She wasn't to be disappointed. No sooner had she reached out to insert the key into the lock than the door abruptly opened before her. Rand stood with one hand still grasping the knob, the other resting impatiently on his upper thigh.

"Do you have any idea what time it is?" he demanded, his tone of voice probably the same one he used to send corporate underlings scurrying like rats to their respective corners.

Jordon pretended to consult her watch, then smiled innocently. "Yes. I believe it's close to one. Does this displease you?"

"It displeases me, Ms. Maxwell," he replied

sarcastically, "to see how little disregard you have for your safety, not to mention the shameful neglect of our children."

For several long minutes Jordon simply stared at him. Her first impulse was to find an object capable of putting a large dent in his obnoxious head and hurling it at him. And yet, she decided as she willed her temper into a more mellow state, the longer she stared at him, the more comical his outburst became.

"I thought we covered the deprived children aspect of this relationship earlier," Jordon remarked off-handedly as she brushed by him and walked into the kitchen. She automatically turned on the stove to heat water for a cup of tea. Knowing that Rand loathed the drink, she didn't bother asking if he would join her. She crossed her arms at her waist, then turned and faced him, slightly taken aback to find him standing directly behind her. For such a large man he was incredibly light on his feet. "I can't live in a locked house for the rest of my life, Rand. And for the life of me I don't understand why you're still so worried."

"That's not surprising," he said furiously. "There are a number of things you don't understand."

"Meaning what?" she asked resignedly, and immediately tuned out his voice. Damn him! She didn't want to fight with him, couldn't he see that? She was quite astonished at how her feelings had grown steadily stronger for Rand. She wanted him to stop his infernal arguing and hold her. She wanted him to kiss her, to run his hands over her body and make her come alive in his arms. Instead, she thought as she stared stonily at him, he was standing in front of her ranting and raving like a braying jackass! Frankly, she reasoned, it looked as if there was nothing wrong with him other than a good healthy dose of jealousy.

That realization rocked Jordon's sense of emotional balance. Jealousy usually indicated that one cared deeply about a person or thing, didn't it? she asked herself. Was it possible that Rand was trying to find his way through a jungle of uncertainties, the same as she was? Could it be possible that he cared for her? He'd acted totally out of character for the Rand she thought she knew. And wasn't it way past time for him to return to Denver?

A warm rush of emotion flooded her being, leaving her feeling curiously vulnerable as a fantasized inkling of what might be floated through her mind.

"Do you understand?" Rand demanded.

"What?" Jordon asked, not having the foggiest notion what he was talking about.

"Didn't you hear a word I said?"

"No," she said frankly.

Rand ran one hand through his hair, his face a scowling mask. "How the hell can I rest easy when you go around with your head in the sand?"

"What on earth are you talking about?" Jordon stormed. She added hot water to a mug already outfitted with a tea bag, then stalked over and sat down at the table, still somewhat bemused by where her thoughts had taken her, but also annoyed with Rand.

"I've just spent at least five minutes telling you my plans for the next week. I have to go back to Denver in the morning. Both Sid and W. C. have been informed of this and have been instructed to keep close to the house. I'm still not ready to let the children get back in the car pool. So let's continue our present arrangements for their transportation to and from school for another couple of weeks."

"Anything else?" Jordon inquired sweetly, though there wasn't the slightest bit of humor in her dark eyes. How was it possible for her to want this man to make love to her one minute, then want to strangle him the next? She was rather positive that she had fallen in love with Rand, and she was equally sure that she would miss him like the very devil when he returned to Denver. But even those two very pertinent facts weren't enough to allow him to treat her as if she didn't have a brain. Maybe it wasn't such a bad idea . . . his leaving the next day, she consoled herself. They both needed a breather.

"There sure as hell is," Rand said impatiently. He whipped out a chair and sat down. "I want you to promise me to be careful while I'm away."

"I am not a two-year-old, Rand," she said curtly, "nor am I indifferent to your fears for our safety. After what's happened, I can certainly understand you feeling the way you do. There are moments when I think of what could have happened, and I become terrified. On the other hand," she went on, "I think you're overreacting by still thinking that me and the children are in danger just because the general public has learned who we are."

"You make me sound like a damn nut," he said, frowning.

Jordon covered his hand with hers and smiled. "You do sound a bit flaky," she agreed, "but I understand why. I think if you really stop and look at the situation, you'll see that I'm right. The reporters have stopped camping across the street from here, we're no longer the topic of the gossip columns, and I've stopped getting calls at the office, asking for a story of our love life. In short, the Maxwells are no longer newsworthy. Isn't that nice?"

Rand studied her broodingly, his fingers idly weaving in and out with hers. "What you say makes sense," he admitted gruffly, "though I'll worry about you and the kids all the same. But that's not all that's bothering me. There's the problem of us."

Jordon dropped her gaze to their hands, which were clasped together. Her heart was lurching like crazy. Was he trying to tell her he wanted things between them back on a purely impersonal basis?

"Don't look so distressed, honey," Rand said quietly. He stood, then reached down and brought Jordon to her feet, folding her tightly into his arms and close to his chest. "I came down here when I heard you were in trouble, with nothing more on my mind than to see that the children had adequate supervision and that you got proper medical attention." He exhaled sharply. "The day I arrived in New Orleans seems like a lifetime ago."

"And during that lifetime?" Jordon whispered.

"During that lifetime," Rand responded, "I've gotten to know the triplets, and I've quit blaming you for the failure of our marriage. I've also come to realize that I want to be a real father to *my* children. And"—he slipped a finger beneath her chin and tipped her head back so that he could see into her face—"I think I'm falling in love with my children's mother. Hopefully this latter state of affairs would account for the crazy way I've been acting lately."

"What do you want the lady to say in response?" Jordon smiled lazily. Dear God, it felt so good being in his arms, being this close to him, feeling his heart beating, seeing things about him she'd never known before. Had she been totally blind seven years ago?

"Right at this moment I want the lady to say yes when I ask her to go with me to my hotel."

Jordon reached out and picked up her purse from where she'd dropped it on the table. "The lady says yes, and you didn't even have to ask the question."

As they turned and walked toward the door

she paused. "I'd better go tell W. C. where I'll be."

"Don't worry," Rand said, sweeping her on out the door on his arm. "I've already taken care of that."

"Pretty sure of yourself, aren't you?" she asked in feigned annoyance.

"Let's say I was hopeful." Rand chuckled. "I was hoping against hope that you were in about the same boat I'm in . . . emotion-wise, that is."

"And if I hadn't been?"

"Then it would have been one hell of a long trip back to Denver in the morning."

The drive to his hotel seemed over before it began. Jordon sat close beside Rand, and they were both strangely quiet. It was as if neither of them was ready to bare their feelings for each other, she told herself. It also seemed to her that they were both being very cautious and apprehensive, knowing the havoc they'd once wrought in each other's lives, and not wanting it to be repeated.

There was only a single lamp burning in the sitting room of Rand's hotel suite, and Jordon barely caught a glimpse of the attractive room before she found herself being caught up in Rand's arms and carried to the bedroom.

Without a word being spoken, they began to undress, each anxious, each hungry, for the feel of the other's body and the release of frustrated passion and desire.

"You're very beautiful." Rand's husky

whisper brought Jordon's gaze up to meet his in the dim light of the room. He'd completed undressing and was watching her, his eyes bathing her with a glow as soft as blue velvet. She kicked away her panty hose, then straightened and reached for the front opening of her bra.

"Let me." He replaced her fingers with his, torturing himself by slowly removing the silken fabric till her full, white breasts were totally visible to him. He brought his hands up and cupped them, the feel of them like satin to his rough palm. With gentle reluctance he released them, his hands eager to invade the entire paradise of her body rather than one spot.

Her thighs opened to his probing fingers. The warm moistness he encountered raised a flicker of pride; he'd read her correctly, Rand thought, relieved. There may be things about Jordon he'd never known, but of one thing he was certain. Her body spoke a language that was plain and simple to him. She wanted him.

His large frame bent forward, and his mouth took a rosy nipple between its lips. As he tugged and teased the tempting morsel he was intensely aware of the faint sounds coming from Jordon. Just as he was aware of her hands stroking his body and lingering on his hips, his thighs, as she tested his readiness.

A hoarse groan burst from Rand's lips. The passion mounting in him had him ready to explode, making him dizzy with wanting Jordon. He gave a slight lunge to one side, and they

161

both landed in a tangle of legs and arms and hands that soon righted themselves as Rand moved into place over Jordon. He entered her swiftly and deeply. There was a need within him to communicate the unsettled state of their relationship to her. He was bothered because they hadn't had the time to work out all the details. He wanted her assurance that there would be no other men in her life while he was away. He wanted her in a way that was baffling to himself. His uncertainties became forged with his inexplicable need for this woman, intensifying the primitive rhythm that caught and held Jordon a willing prisoner within its force.

Afterward Jordon lay with her head on Rand's chest, running the pads of her fingers over the hair-roughened skin. "There was something special about it tonight," she murmured, almost as an afterthought. She had truly felt as if she were dying . . . and she had welcomed it.

"I know," Rand replied quietly. "Seems like it couldn't possibly be better between two people, doesn't it?"

"I don't see how," she agreed, catching only the briefest hesitancy in his voice.

"But it has to be for the right reasons, doesn't it?" And Jordon knew then that he wasn't referring only to their having made love. Suddenly he moved, placing Jordon on her back and propping himself beside her on one elbow, his other hand possessively cupping a breast. "I'm having the damnedest time trying to separate *this* Jordon"—his hand tightened on her breast—"from the one I used to know. I also have to be sure my motives are different. Can you understand that?"

All Jordon could actually see in the dim light was the outline of his head and shoulders as he leaned over her. But she didn't need a burst of sunlight to read the seriousness of his tone. Rand had always put her welfare first. Even when he thought her unfaithful to him, he hadn't quibbled about supporting the triplets. When he heard of the incident in the grocery store, he'd come to her rescue again. "Yes," she said slowly, "I understand." Then she smiled. "Think of all the poor people in the world who have ordinary, uneventful, boring relationships."

"There's one thing of which I'm certain, Ms. Maxwell," he rasped huskily as he dipped his head and teased a nipple with the tip of his tongue.

"What's that?" Jordan asked, reacting to the caress with a burst of desire that rushed to the ends of her toes and back.

"The ritual of making love may be ordinary to some people, sweetheart, but you are fantastic." His mouth covered hers, his tongue plundering the softness it found. Jordon's fingers clutched his shoulders, her fingernails biting into his skin as desire and passion ripped its way through her veins and left her begging him to take her.

* * *

"What can I do to help?" Jordon asked W. C. as she walked into the kitchen, the aroma of pot roast tickling her nose. It was still early, but true to her word to Rand, she'd gotten home daily at least thirty minutes ahead of her usual schedule. Rand had been gone for five days, and she missed him terribly.

"The butter and the rolls are ready, and also the peas." W. C. nodded. "Have you heard from the boss today?"

"He called this morning, but I was out," Jordon answered between trips to the table. "I tried returning his call, but by then *he* was out. He'll probably call later this evening. That way he can talk with the kids."

W. C. smiled. "He seems quite taken with the little tykes, doesn't he?"

"Yes, he does," she agreed. "And they with him. It's hard to believe that they've really only known him for such a short time. One would think the triplets had been with him since they were born."

"In my opinion, madam," the portly butler-cum-housekeeper ventured, "their acceptance of Mr. Maxwell was entirely due to the fact that you always presented him to them as a vital part of their young lives. I think it's very admirable of you to have done such a thing."

"Er . . . thank you, W. C.," Jordon murmured. Privately she was thinking how far from the truth he was. Anything admirable about her past exploits to get Rand to recognize his

164

children was purely accidental. She looked over the number of places at the table. "Isn't Sid eating with us?"

"I believe Sidney has a previous engagement with a certain Mrs. Lofts," W. C. informed her.

"Ah ha." Jordon nodded, her eyes gleaming. "If Sid isn't careful, Mrs. Lofts will have him as her permanent yard man."

"Precisely what I told him this morning, madam, though I can't say that he took me seriously. You may call the little ones now, madam."

After dinner, as Jordon had said, Rand did call the children. She stood by smiling as each of the triplets had his or her turn, and naturally they got into a fight with each exchange of the receiver. When the last one was through, Jordon took the phone and dropped back on her bed. "I tried to call you back today, Mr. Maxwell," she said crisply. "Where were you?"

"Afraid I was chasing skirts, Ms. Maxwell?" Rand chuckled.

"Yes. You are a very sexy gentleman. You're also single and wealthy. A woman would be a fool not to have a go at you, you know."

"I'll remember that. But what about you, Jordon? How have you been spending your evenings?" The question was asked lightly, but nothing could hide the thread of steel underneath.

"With two men," she said, teasing.

"Which two?" Rand snapped, his voice like the flicking of a rawhide whip.

"Sid and W. C. Who else? I have breakfast and dinner with them. Does that please you?" she asked dryly.

"Immensely. Don't make any plans for tomorrow evening," he added. "I'll be returning to New Orleans shortly after lunch."

"Oh? For how long?" It seemed a casual enough question, but Jordon knew that his answer was one of the most important things in the world to her.

"Long enough for us to get our relationship sorted out, honey. I've missed you like hell." Rand's voice sounded warm and urgent in her ear, and Jordon would have given anything to be in his arms.

After their conversation Jordon went to help the kids with their homework, then gave them their baths and put them to bed. Some time later she dropped wearily into a chair in the living room, her gaze automatically going to the television screen. For a moment she couldn't get the gist of what the announcer was saying, then she recognized two of the five faces taken from mug shots being flashed across the screen. She sat frozen, unable to believe her eyes.

They'd done it again! Two of the crazy idiots who had held her hostage had escaped, along with three other men.

The next afternoon a very annoyed Jordon stood listening to a Detective Johnson while a very tense featured Rand sat on the edge of her desk.

"These things happen, Ms. Maxwell." The detective shrugged. "We're sorry, but at this point there's little we can do, other than the protection we've offered you."

"How about Mr. Bradford, the store manager, and Mr. Mason?" she asked. "Have you spoken with them?"

"Yes, we have, and each of them accepted. Now, with Mr. Maxwell"—he nodded toward Rand—"volunteering to move in with you, I feel a lot easier." Privately he was dying to know exactly what their relationship was, but courtesy prevented him from asking. He turned to go. "Call me if the slightest thing out of the ordinary comes up. I'll be in touch." He gave them a resigned nod and left.

Once they were alone, Jordon turned and stared incredulously at Rand. "Can you believe it? Ralph and Elmer! Those two bungling idiots managing to break out of jail. I think I'm losing my mind."

Rand shook his head slowly. "I must admit that they do seem to have about as many lives as a cat." He dropped his palms against his thighs and looked around the office. "Can you leave now?"

Jordon glanced around and nodded. "I suppose so. Give me a minute or two to go over a couple of things with Gloria." She grabbed a file and hurried over to one of two desks in the front of the office where an attractive blonde was sitting.

Rand watched the movement of Jordon's slender body and realized again just how much he loved her. During the week he'd been away from her, she barely left his thoughts. He'd stayed at the desk in his impressive Denver office from morning till close to midnight each day. But no matter how hard he worked or how weary he was, Jordon's face stayed front and foremost in his mind. He missed her like hell during the day, and his nights were empty shells as he tossed and turned until exhaustion overtook him in the form of fitful sleep.

He watched her coming toward him, a sense of pride overtaking him. It struck him all of a sudden. She belonged to him now.

"Why are you smiling?" Jordon asked when she got within arm's length of him.

"I was just thinking of something that turned out exceptionally well for me," he said smoothly. "Something I'd invested rather heavily in." He picked up her purse and handed it to her. "Shall we go?"

Jordon didn't question his comment. Her mind was taken over with this latest upheaval in her life. How on earth could the police have been so careless as to let two lunatics escape? she asked herself for the tenth or so time. It simply didn't make sense.

Rand, seeing the expression of bewilderment on her face as they drove home, dropped a hand to her shoulder and squeezed. "Don't worry, Jordon. Everything's going to work out all right. You said it yourself: Those characters are idiots. The police will have them back in custody in no time."

She threw back her head and lifted her hands defeatedly. "Oh, I suppose you're right. It's just that I resent the fact that some lowlife can disrupt our lives without a care in the world. We're at their misguided mercy. Can you beat that?"

Her fiery temper amused Rand. He was well aware of the danger the jailbreak could hold, but he reserved that fear for himself. He wasn't leaving Jordon's side, and in order to get to her, something or someone would have to come through him.

"This is completely changing the subject, but would you mind if Lindsey came down for a visit?"

"I think it would be very nice. After all, other than you and me, she is the triplets' only living relative," Jordon said thoughtfully. "From what little I saw of your sister I liked her. I felt then that she would be better off away from you, but that's her business."

"Lindsey's shy."

"You are overbearing. That's what makes Lindsey shy," Jordon said spiritedly. "Your daughter is shy, but she doesn't hesitate to clobber either of her brothers if they do something mean to her. Try to think of Lindsey in that light, and consider letting her live her own life for a change."

169

Rand turned his head and glared at her. "Has anyone ever told you that you are a busy-body?"

"Of course." She smiled, ignoring his barb. She let her head rest against the back of the seat and closed her eyes. Rand was back. That made her world complete . . . in spite of Ralph and Elmer lurking about! "Has the great jailbreak of the century canceled our dinner plans?"

"Not on your life."

"Great. Expecting the worst at any moment has given me a tremendous appetite."

Rand chuckled, then slipped an arm around her and pulled her close to him. "That's what I like about you, Jordon, you're so sensitive," he said, teasing. "I remember seeing that same streak in Chad when Jon cut his finger."

"Smart kid to take after his mother."

"Well, since Mandy takes after Lindsey, and Chad takes after you, does that mean Jon has been lucky enough to inherit all my charming and adorable traits?" he asked teasingly. Jordon took up the gauntlet, and they continued the carefree banter all the way home and afterward. They were happy, and it showed in their actions and their faces.

A few hours later a barefoot Rand passed Jordon in the hall. He had on nothing but a pair of jeans, and the sight of his broad, tanned shoulders caused Jordon to suck in her breath. She was in faded jeans and an old shirt. He'd been working on the bookcase in the boys' room, and his hands were full of tools.

"Chop-chop, toots," he said, leering lasciviously as they passed. "Our reservations are for seven-thirty. That only gives you about an hour and a half."

"When one is as beautiful as I," Jordon countered dramatically, her nose in the air, "one needs only mere seconds to be transformed into a ravishing vamp."

Rand's "That's a laugh" could be heard through the house and brought a delighted chuckle from W. C., who was busy arranging his employer's things in Mandy's closet. Sleeping arrangements were still a bit vague, but W. C. didn't mind. Things were working out quite nicely, he thought. It wouldn't be long now before Mrs. Maxwell and the little tykes would be joining them in Denver.

As Jordon walked through her bedroom to the adjoining bath to put away some towels just out of the dryer, a flash of color from the window caught her eye: The yellow and white fall mums she'd planted three years ago, the heavy blossoms almost bending the bushes to the ground. A bouquet would be beautiful on the breakfast-room table, she decided.

Disregarding the fact that she had precious little time to waste cutting flowers for bouquets, Jordon hurried to the kitchen, grabbed a pair of shears and a basket, then scooted out the door. Seconds later she was humming hap-

171

pily as she bent over to snip a lovely yellow mum.

Then a rough hand slid over her mouth!

Jordon tried to scream, but the sound became a gurgling noise in her throat. She tried to use the shears as a weapon, but they were knocked from her hand. An arm clamped her waist, and Jordon felt herself being pulled backward toward a row of tall hedges that separated her property from that of her neighbor. She began struggling with all her might, kicking and twisting for dear life.

A muttered "Ouch!" sounded from her assailant.

Jordon froze. She wanted to scream out in frustration but was able to manage only a strangled grunt. Even without looking, she knew the idiot abducting her was Ralph . . . exalted leader of the "gang" that had held up the grocery and left her with two gunshot wounds to the head. This couldn't be happening. Not two times in her life. Surely the law of averages had something to say about such a dirty trick being played on a person.

She renewed her struggle. Ralph cried out in pain when her elbow made contact with his solar plexus.

"Elmer!" he hissed in as loud a voice as he dared. "Get off your ass and come over here and help me. She's worse than a damn cat."

A cat was right, Jordon swore silently, scratching and kicking for all she was worth. One part of her mind registered the slamming of a car door and the starting of an engine. She recognized the sound as her neighbor's car.

Oh, please, she prayed silently, *let them see me. Let them see these two weird-looking men dragging me across my side lawn. Let them call Rand.* But there were no voices raised in alarm, nor any sign of Rand's powerful body knocking away her attackers and sweeping her safely up into his arms.

"Dammit, Ralph!" Elmer swore. "I told you let's go after that store manager feller." He met Jordon's angry gaze and gave a start when she tried to lunge at him. "She's meaner than hell."

"She's also got an old man that's richer than hell. What do you think about that?"

Elmer scratched his chin with one skinny finger, only slightly more pleased. "I don't know, Ralph. If I had a woman as mean as this one here, damned if I'd pay to get her back."

"Well, her old man will," Ralph snapped. "Now get that car we stole and ease it up to where them bushes end by the street. We got to get out of here."

CHAPTER TEN

Rand stood at the table, his hands braced on its edges, his shoulders hunched as he stared at the shears and the basket that had been found in the side yard, Detective Johnson's voice going on in the background as he spoke with headquarters.

"Try not to worry so, sir," W. C. said, trying to comfort his employer. "I'm sure Mrs. Maxwell will be just fine. I've often heard her say that she really didn't think those men who tried to rob the grocery store were violent—just stupid and careless."

"That's just the point, W. C.," Rand said in a cold, distant voice. "We can't be sure exactly who abducted Jordon. If Ralph and Elmer split from the other three and *are* the ones who have her, then that's a little better . . . only slightly better. However, if they shot off their mouth to those other three characters and told them Jordon's connection with me, then it's a whole different ball game."

"Some good news," Detective Johnson said briskly as he returned to where Rand was standing. "Two of the five have been recaptured. The police found them hiding underneath an overpass among some parked cars. Seems Ralph and Elmer went their own way, as did the other character." He pocketed his worn notepad, then gave Rand and W. C. a wan smile. "I'm on my way to headquarters now to question the two that have been picked up. If I hear anything about your wife, I'll let you know. You do the same. Frankly I'm as surprised as you are that those two yo-yos could get as close as they did." He shrugged. "See you later."

"Thanks, Johnson," Rand muttered without ever looking up. He was barely aware of W. C. showing the officer to the door. Never in his life had Rand felt so desolate . . . so alone. It was as if his life had come to a complete stop. Without Jordon he had nothing.

"What about the children, sir?" W. C. asked as he entered the room. "What should we tell them if their mother isn't here by morning?"

"What?" Rand stared puzzledly at him for several seconds. What the hell was he talking about? Then it hit him.

God! The children. Certainly they would have to be told something. He continued to stare at the Englishman, at a complete loss. "I'm not sure, W. C.," he finally admitted. He walked over and poured himself a cup of coffee, unmindful that it burned his mouth with the first sip.

She'd gone after a damned bouquet of flowers and they'd grabbed her. He felt the stron-

gest urge to go out and dynamite the flowers
. . . anything to get rid of this feeling of helplessness. He was a man accustomed to action.
When he spoke, his employees listened or their
heads rolled. Being forced to wait for an over-
weight detective in a rumpled suit was something Rand was finding difficult to accept.

"If you like, sir, I'll take care of the little
ones," W. C. said, trying again.

"No," Rand said decisively. "If we don't
have any news by morning, then I'll handle it.
It'll have to be something believable, though.
They're not dummies." A soft prickle of pride
ran through him. They were Jordon's children
. . . and his, he proudly acknowledged, and
she had raised them to be strong.

"I'm hungry, Ralph," Elmer complained for
the third or fourth time in less than an hour.
"Let's stop and eat."

"And what, may I ask, should we use for
money?" Ralph snarled furiously at his accom-
plice.

"I'm hungry too," Jordon piped up from the
backseat. So far, all they'd done was drive
around the city in large, sweeping circles. From
what she could make of their constant wran-
gling, they didn't seem to have any specific
plan in mind . . . other than extorting money
from Rand.

"She's hungry too," Elmer repeated. "When
are we going to get all that money from her old
man, Ralph? Can we do it tonight? I remember

watching a television show one time. They gave the man back his boy, and he gave them the money. Why don't we do that?"

"We will," Ralph agreed. "But we've got to figure out a place to meet before we call him."

"How much do you think we'll get?" Elmer asked excitedly. "Can we go to Mexico?"

"Yeah. But first let's buy us some new duds." Ralph threw Jordon a quick glance, satisfied that her hands and feet were still tied. "How much do you figure your old man will pay to get you back?"

"He's not my old man," Jordon told him again. "We're divorced. Can't we please stop for a while? These ropes are giving me blisters." This time she was not nearly as worried about being shot as before. There seemed to be only one gun, and Ralph was carrying it. Elmer was unhappy about that; Jordon definitely wasn't.

"You hush!" Elmer said sternly, clearly annoyed that he couldn't eat. "You're our hostage. You can't ask for anything."

"Well, there's no reason to blister her all up, Elmer," Ralph said, speaking up. "Besides, I'm the boss, and I say loosen the ropes." He pulled into a dark alleyway, then turned and leaned over the back of the front seat. In minutes Jordon could feel a tingling sensation as the feeling began to return to her feet.

"Thank you," she said wearily. "Where are we staying tonight?"

"Don't tell her anything, Ralph," Elmer

warned. "She might have some of that wire on her."

Both men turned and looked at her, suspicion bright in their eyes. "What kind of wire?" Ralph asked in a hushed voice, and in spite of the precariousness of her situation, it was all Jordon could do not to laugh.

"Do you?" Ralph threw the question at her, his round face scrunched up like a bulldog's.

"What?"

"Are you wired up like Elmer said?"

"No," she said with a sigh. "People don't just walk around with recording devices taped to their bodies. You only see that on TV."

"See?" Ralph punched Elmer on the shoulder. "I didn't think there was anything to that."

As the argument between the two men continued, Jordan was racking her brain, trying to come up with a way to escape. It seemed about the only thing she could do was to encourage them to get a note to Rand or call him as soon as possible. She didn't think they would hurt her, but she couldn't trust them, either. Elmer was extremely simple-minded, with no sense of reasoning, she decided. Ralph appeared to be a little more reliable. Up to this point neither had seemed violent, discounting the shooting incident at the grocery store. She sincerely hoped it continued that way.

"Well, look in the glove compartment," Ralph was saying when Jordan began paying attention to their conversation. "Surely you can find something."

"What are you looking for?" she asked curiously.

"Don't tell her, Ralph." Elmer frowned.

"Hush, Elmer." He turned to Jordon. "I need something to write down your phone number on."

"Why?"

"So we can get a million dollars from . . ." Elmer frowned, then looked at Ralph. "If they're not married, what are they?"

"How the hell would I know?" Ralph scowled. "Anyway, she's just telling us that about being divorced. Remember me telling you about reading all them stories in the newspapers about them. Why, they got three young-uns."

Elmer nodded. "They're married, then." He handed Ralph a small piece of paper and a pen. He looked back at Jordon. "Give Ralph your man's number."

She did, then waited. Her mind was still reeling that such a thing had happened to her. She thought of the children. They were just now getting their lives back to normal after her previous ordeal with Ralph and Elmer and their three comrades. Now they were quite likely to be thrown for another loss by this latest development.

Jordon wondered about Rand. Her love for him was so strong. Even at that moment, trussed up as she was and sitting in a dark alley and not knowing what was going to happen to her, thoughts of him warmed her heart and gave her hope. Rand was a fighter. He would gain her release or die trying.

Suddenly the car began to move, and Jordon tensed. "Where are we going?"

"To find a phone booth. We've got to get hold of some money," Ralph informed her.

"Don't forget something to eat," Elmer chimed in just as the car gave a chug-chugging noise and rolled to a dead stop.

"Now what?" Ralph yelled. He turned and glared at Elmer. "You're supposed to be a mechanic. Do something!"

"What?" a perplexed Elmer asked.

"Fix it!"

Elmer opened the door cautiously, peering left and right before stepping out onto the pavement and walking around to the front of the car. Jordon saw Ralph lean forward and pull the hood release.

After several minutes, during which a continuous battle raged between the two, Elmer announced that he didn't know what was wrong. In spite of being warned repeatedly to lie down and not sit, Jordon managed to twist around so that she could see out the front. If she didn't help these two loonies, there was no telling what they would get into. She did not want to be on foot for any length of time with Ralph and Elmer. She glanced at the lighted dash and found the reading for the fuel.

"There's nothing wrong with the car, Ralph. You're out of gas."

That brought on another clash between

Ralph and Elmer, with Ralph deciding that since Elmer was so stupid as to steal a car with only a few gallons of gas in it, he should be the one to go find a phone booth.

That didn't please Jordon at all. She'd rather the three of them stayed together. They'd be more conspicuous, she figured, if they were lucky enough to run into a policeman, and it would give her a chance to keep Ralph and Elmer at odds with each other. She'd decided that would be the only way she could escape.

"Why don't we all go?" she suggested. She looked out the window and shuddered. "This isn't the safest place for us to wait. Somebody might slip up on us and knock us in the head, Ralph."

She saw the expression of fear in both their eyes. They each threw guarded looks over their shoulders and then held a mumbled conversation. A sigh of relief escaped Jordon when she saw Ralph turn and lean over the seat and began removing the rough pieces of rope around her wrists and ankles.

"Don't be gettin any ideas," he warned her. "My gun's in my belt. You walk between us, and don't act crazy. Understand?"

Jordon nodded, eager to get out in the open. Surely the police would be looking for them. All she had to do now was steer them toward a better section of town where there would be more people, consequently more uniforms.

As usual with Ralph and Elmer, her suggestion was met with instant war. Fortunately for

Jordon, though, they walked as they argued, and she more or less began leading them toward more lights and people.

When a phone booth was spotted, Ralph rushed toward it, pulling Jordon in his wake. He opened the door, reached for the receiver, then paused. A look of perplexity stealing over his face. "We don't have any money."

"Well, even if we did have," Elmer sang out, "there ain't no place to put it. That's the funniest telephone I've ever seen."

"They're used mainly for making long-distance calls. Let me try. I'll give them my credit card number."

"Wait a minute," Elmer said roughly.

"Shut up!" Ralph snarled. "Let her make the call. That way we can get our money and get her off our hands. I'm tired of her tagging along."

Jordon literally held her breath as the operator came on the line and she gave her the information needed. When she heard Rand's deep voice before the first ring had ended, she slumped against the side of the booth in relief. "Rand?" she said hurriedly. "I'm all right. I—" the receiver was yanked roughly from her hand, and Ralph began to talk, demanding a huge ransom and setting up a place for the exchange.

Soon it would be daylight, Jordon thought as she stood on the littered sidewalk and leaned against the brick wall. Ralph and Elmer were directly behind her, inside the abandoned building. They had placed her between a window and the door. There was nothing but abandoned buildings and warehouses in the area, and Jordon was frightened. Although, she thought, it was a perfect location for Ralph and Elmer. It was the only sensible decision they'd made since kidnapping Jordon.

A sound caught her ear. She turned and looked to her right, squinting in order to see better in the fog that was rolling in. Soon everything would be blanketed in a gray sheet of mist. Including herself, she sighed.

There was another sound. She cocked her head and listened. This time she saw movement. Not much; just enough to let her know that someone was near.

She froze. There was no doubt in her mind that Rand would bring help. There was also no doubt in her mind that Ralph and Elmer would be recaptured. They honestly believed that once they'd released her, Rand would supply them with the outrageous amount they'd asked as ransom and the authorities would stand calmly by and allow them to leave the country.

There was more movement, too much for it to be a coincidence, Jordon decided. She saw a car turn down the street that was crisscrossed with the iron rails of train tracks. The car stopped, and a man got out. Even at that distance Jordon knew it was Rand.

She was dying to run.

"Don't be gettin any idea 'bout running out

on us," Ralph hissed in her ear. He'd eased out and was standing beside her. One hand grasped her elbow.

Jordon watched Rand coming closer and closer. The strain she'd been under for the past few hours began to show. She could feel perspiration breaking out across her forehead and down the middle of her back. When Rand reached a certain point, Ralph yelled for him to stop.

He motioned for Elmer to step out. "Go get a look inside that briefcase he's carrying. If you see green, I'll let her go. If you don't, I'll shoot her."

Jordon's heart dropped to her feet. It was the first genuine threat that had been made to her. She felt the cold, hard steel of the gun against her ribs as she watched Elmer approach Rand.

She saw Rand open the case, saw Elmer lean forward, then heard him exclaim, "Hot doggies!" He turned back to Ralph. "It's here."

Ralph gave Jordon a sudden, hard push that almost sent her to the ground. "Go on. Get," he yelled, his eyes as bright as a little child's on Christmas morning.

Her feet literally flew across the asphalt, past a grinning Elmer, and into Rand's arms. Her face was buried against his chest, and she could feel the vibrations of his heart and its forceful pounding.

"Let's get the hell out of here, sweetheart," he murmured in her ear. He caught her hand

and began running back to the car. Once there, he practically threw her inside on the driver's side and slid in behind her.

"Is there going to be trouble?" she asked as she held on for dear life while Rand made a tight turn and burned rubber leaving the scene.

"That place is surrounded by police. They'll have them back in custody before long. I was afraid they would get to examining the money before we left."

"What's wrong with it?"

"The majority of it is play money," Rand told her. "There was no way in hell I could have raised the amount of cash they were asking for in the middle of the night."

"Play money is what those two deserve." Jordon sighed. She leaned against Rand's arm, feeling really safe for the first time in hours. "They are the most incredibly stupid people on God's green earth. I couldn't believe my ears when I heard the deal they made with you." She looked up at him. "Would you believe I even had to pay for my own ransom call?" Then she explained about the phone.

Rand laughed, more out of relief than any real amusement. He felt like he'd aged twenty years in a few hours. The police had assured him that Ralph and Elmer had never been violent, but he'd worried just the same. Now the worry was over, and he was weak with relief.

He hugged her tight to his chest, his chin

buried in her hair. "You owe me one, Ms. Maxwell."

"Name it," Jordon said softly.

"I want a week alone with you. Starting today."

"But, Rand," she cried. "There are the children, my work, the—"

"All of which can be looked after by others," he said firmly. "Sid, Ellie, W. C., and Lindsey will take care of the children, and you have perfectly capable help at the office, so you really have no excuse for not going with me."

"I'm not sure I'd know how to act with a whole week ahead of me with nothing to do," she murmured, warming to the idea already.

"Even if you were to take on the responsibility of being my wife?"

The question caught Jordon off-guard. She sat quietly, not sure that she'd heard correctly. "Rand?" she looked at him, her eyes questioning.

"Please marry me," he whispered, then gave a muttered "Damn!" as the right tires of the car struck the curb. He switched off the engine with a chuckle. "You'd better say yes before I wreck the car and kill us."

"For the right reasons this time, Rand?" she asked honestly, the love in her heart shining in her face.

"For all the right reasons, Jordon," he repeated.

"I love you, Rand Maxwell. With all my heart and soul."

"And I love you, Jordon Maxwell. You're my life."

Tears came to Jordon's eyes as she was folded in his strong arms. Through the bleary mist she saw the sudden brilliance of the sun as it struggled to make its first appearance of the day. It was a new day for her and for her love for Rand, Jordon thought. A new day and a new life.